Thoroughbred Legacy
The stakes are high.

Scandal has hit the Australian branch
of the Preston family. Find out what it will take
to return this horse-racing dynasty to the winner's circle!

Available December 2008

#9 *Darci's Pride* by Jenna Mills
Six years ago, Tyler Preston's passion nearly cost him everything.
Now he's rebuilt his stables *and* his reputation, only to find the
woman he once loved walking back into his life.

#10 *Breaking Free* by Loreth Anne White
Aussie cop Dylan Hastings believes in things that are *real*.
Family. Integrity. Justice. In his experience, the wrong woman
can destroy it all. So when Megan Stafford comes to town,
he knows trouble's not far behind.

#11 *An Indecent Proposal* by Margot Early
Widowed, penniless and desperate,
Bronwyn Davies came to Fairchild Acres looking for work—and
to confront her son's real father. This time she'll show her lover
exactly what she's made of…and what he's been missing!

#12 *The Secret Heiress* by Bethany Campbell
After her mother's dying confession,
Marie walks away from her life and her career…only to
find herself next door to racing-world royalty. Wealthy
Andrew Preston may make Marie feel like Cinderella, but
she knows men like Andrew don't fall for women like her.…

W9-AVS-233

Dear Reader,

It has been a real pleasure to take part in the THOROUGHBRED LEGACY continuity series. I love working with characters who are interconnected, whose lives branch out in so many ways. It echoes life, in that everything we say and do matters and touches others.

Though I enjoyed getting to know Patrick, Bronwyn and especially Wesley, the character who most intrigued me was matriarch Louisa Fairchild. I love that she is able to share her life experience with Bronwyn—and that this influences the choices Bronwyn makes. Also, it was fun to be able to introduce Marie LaFayette, whom you will get to know better in the next book. She is a woman of heart; I can't wait to know her secrets.

I wish you great joy in reading the last books in this series—as much delight as I hope you experienced reading the earlier stories. To you, all good things.

Sincerely,

Margot Early

Thoroughbred Legacy

AN INDECENT PROPOSAL

Margot Early

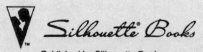

Silhouette Books

Published by Silhouette Books

America's Publisher of Contemporary Romance

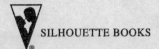

SILHOUETTE BOOKS

®

ISBN-13: 978-0-373-19936-5
ISBN-10:   0-373-19936-8

AN INDECENT PROPOSAL

Special thanks and acknowledgment are given to Margot Early
for her contribution to the Thoroughbred Legacy series.

Printed in U.S.A.

MARGOT EARLY

has written stories since she was twelve years old. She has sold 3.6 million books published with Harlequin. Her work has been translated into nine languages and sold in sixteen countries. Ms. Early lives high in Colorado's San Juan Mountains with two German shepherds and several other pets, including snakes and tarantulas. She enjoys the outdoors, dance and spinning dog hair.

ACKNOWLEDGMENTS

Special thanks to Catherine Cockburn,
who read this manuscript for Australian authenticity;
also to Catherine and her husband Keith for being
lovely hosts to me here in Colorado.
All errors in this fictional work are mine.

Chapter One

It was hot, a March hot where the heat came up from the bitumen in visible waves. Bronwyn and ten-year-old Wesley rode in the front of an ancient Toyota truck—no air-conditioning—and it was broiling. Bronwyn's straight dark red hair blew dankly around her face, her skin stuck to her khaki slacks and the ripped vinyl upholstery, and Wesley was crying.

He was crying about Ari of course. Because Ari was dead. The only father Wesley had ever known had been in prison for his involvement with a crime syndicate. He'd been murdered in prison.

Sweltering, and certain the Vietnamese driver of the Toyota had emigrated too recently to have much

English, Bronwyn spoke freely. "Please don't waste another tear on him, Wesley," she told him, which wasn't something she would have said if her once-white blouse hadn't been pasted to her body with sweat, if they hadn't spent almost an hour crawling behind another ute on the winding road with no chance to overtake. Instead, she couldn't restrain the impulse to tell her only son not to mourn Aristotle. "In fact," she added, "it's his fault we're in this fix. It's his fault you have to move away from your friends and go to a new school." Once again, nothing she'd have said most days.

She spared a look at the tearful boy and past him to the driver. Mr. Le at the Asian market in Sydney had found this man for her and imparted the information that his name was Nam and he would drive the three hours to the Hunter Valley, her destination. Wesley sat wedged in the middle of the front seat between Bronwyn and Nam, head down. His hair was lighter than Ari's and without even a hint of Bronwyn's auburn. Nor were his eyes like Ari's dark chocolate ones; they were hazel, not Bronwyn's green. *Just those wild recessive genes, Ari.*

Yes.

Wesley held his soccer ball in his lap. He wore his shin guards and cleats and a child-size Socceroos jersey. He had others, as well, other teams, other countries. His dream was to be a professional soccer player. Better than a footballer, in Bronwyn's opinion, even if Ari had owned a football team. Wesley had picked up the soccer thing from Ari, who had bought him a child-size Manchester United uniform. In any case, Bronwyn had never wanted to discourage her son's dreams and now regretted that he was going to have to experience practicality the hard way. Not as hard as the way *she'd* learned as a child, though.

"And," she continued, forgetting that she'd meant to comfort him, "your last name is Davies."

"It's not." He spoke under his breath, but Bronwyn heard.

"Look, Wesley," she burst out. "I know this isn't fun, but we're going to a place full of people who are probably willing to die for their horses, and I'd rather not share the last name of a man who is known to have been involved with doping them."

"What does doping mean?"

"Giving them drugs. So they'll lose or win or—I don't know. But I *do* know that the name Theodoros is not going to be a passport to anyone's friendship at Fairchild Acres."

Wesley bounced his soccer ball on his knee, and Bronwyn put her hand on top of it. "Don't do that. You'll cause an accident."

"Daddy doesn't have anything to do with the horses at the racetrack. He told me."

"Yes, well, I don't mean it was him personally, and that's only one aspect of his business. Ari was a criminal. He stole money, he cheated the government and he was involved in a lot of unpleasant things you don't need to know about." Bronwyn sincerely hoped Wesley would give up his hero worship of Ari without further examples of his perfidy. If it had been possible, she would have made a priority of protecting her son's image of the man he regarded as father.

However, there had been too many explanations to make. How they had lost their home, cars, planes, bank accounts as law enforcement officials tried to untangle the web of criminal activity in which Ari had been involved. She didn't hate Ari. She didn't mourn him, either. Not now. She hadn't the leisure. Leisure was gone, replaced with indigence.

And she'd sworn she would never be poor again.

Well, the joke was on her, but she'd grown up learning to survive on nothing. If she was angry now it was at herself for ever depending on anyone but Bronwyn Davies.

Now she was back to her maiden name but with complications she'd never had before she was married. Ari was dead, and Bronwyn Davies was glad for the simplification that offered in her own life. She was no longer married, need not obtain a divorce. Which was good. She barely had money to feed herself and her ten-year-old son. She did not have money for attorneys, for messy court battles. When Ari had first been arrested weeks earlier, she'd never considered divorce. In sickness, in health, in deceit and all that. But she'd grown tired of trying to offer Wesley meaningful explanations for things she would never understand: *Why is my father a criminal? Why did he do bad things?*

Just the thought of these questions made her tired.

I can't think about Ari. I can't think about some lag sticking him in prison. I can't think about his face. Too many lies, not all of them his.

"I'm sorry, Wesley. I know you hate this, but you've got to trust me. This is how we need to keep ourselves safe. I know you love Ari—" the words *your father* definitely stuck in her throat "—and that's fine, but we have to be practical."

"We have to lie," Wesley clarified.

Bronwyn wanted to swear. Now *she* was providing the duplicitous example. Also, it alarmed her how rapidly Wesley was becoming a cynic. It was one thing for her to be cynical; she had grown up sometimes literally homeless in Sydney because of poverty and had just discovered after ten-plus years of marriage that her husband's actual job description was "gangster." It was different when the cynic was Wesley, who was such a brave kid, ultimately, who wasn't a whiner or a crybaby.

"This is going to be an adventure," she told him. "You'll like it."

Bronwyn could have said, *What would your dad think if he saw you crying?* That would have stopped those tears in their tracks. Because, of course, Aristotle Theodoros had not tolerated tears in his male child. The child he'd believed to be his flesh and blood.

Well, Bronwyn had been repaid for her own deception now. Touché and all that. Which, after all, was the bigger marital betrayal? Maintaining a double life as a mobster or telling your husband that he was the father of a child who, even at birth, looked eerily like Patrick Stafford? A child who *was* Patrick Stafford's son, not Aristotle Theodoros's.

Then, Bronwyn spotted the first of the white fences and long green fields. Horse country, the Hunter Valley, home of Fairchild Acres, home of Louisa Fairchild and current residence of her great-nephew, Patrick Stafford.

"Wesley, look at the horses. Look how beautiful it is here. You'll see. You'll like living out here. Look at all that grass." She cast a meaningful glance at his soccer ball, though she had no idea if her son would be allowed to play on the grass.

Beside her, Wesley said, for at least the tenth time that day, "I don't like horses."

Patrick Stafford gazed out the French doors of Louisa Fairchild's blue brick Colonial house. Most of the homes in the valley were lowset, but not Fairchild Acres. The sprawling, graceful homestead was very different from the penthouse apartment where he'd grown up in Sydney with his parents. They had been stockbrokers, and Patrick had vowed to do something more meaningful with his life. Yet he'd ended up…a stockbroker. That was all right. He'd lost some romantic ideals along the way, become more pragmatic in general, and he was glad to be able to help people with their finances, as he was helping Louisa.

"Patrick, are you listening to me?" his great-aunt said now.

"Yes, yes." Of course he was. When he'd first come to Fairchild Acres a month earlier, he'd been keen to confront Louisa, to demand answers; he'd wanted to know why she'd mistreated her sister, his grandmother. But gradually, he'd grown to love this elderly woman, as had his sister, Megan. When Louisa had been accused of murdering Sam Whittleson, he'd been outraged. An eighty-year-old woman kill a man she knew, a neighbor? He hadn't believed it. And Louisa had been proven innocent, though the stress of her arrest had sent her into cardiac arrest, something she was quicker to forgive than he was.

His sister, Megan, now planned to spend her life with the arresting officer, Dylan Hastings. Yes, Patrick saw that both Dylan's own misconceptions about Louisa and the orders of his superiors had led to his persecution of the older woman. But still! And now Megan was living with Dylan and his daughter and was planning to open a gallery and artists' retreat.

So his own struggle was to release the last of his anger over offenses against Louisa that she herself had already forgiven.

In any case, this morning he had other preoccupations. While ordinarily he was the most attentive of listeners, today he kept thinking of the morning's news. Just a recap of the events of the past month. Aristotle Theodoros had been murdered in prison two weeks earlier, and speculation was rife that he'd been killed to prevent him testifying against the Syndicate.

It had nothing to do with Patrick—not really. He'd met Ari briefly once, after Bronwyn had told Patrick of her engagement. It seemed a hundred years ago now. To Patrick, Ari had been the man Bronwyn chose over him. The man whose money she'd chosen over his lack thereof, no matter what else she'd claimed. Her rejection had put an end to his plans to do some graduate work in history, some writing, nebulous dreams.

He realized now he'd never been a writer.

He'd been born with his parents' fine-tuned instincts for the stock market. They'd died when he was eighteen, but they'd left him and Megan comfortable. His university goals had reflected that ease, he supposed. It had taken a shallow woman's ridiculing his dreams to make him see his own future clearly.

Well, *hers* certainly hadn't worked out. Aristotle Theodoros's assets had been seized, and Patrick would have needed the soul of a saint not to enjoy the irony. Weeks earlier, he had caught one glimpse of Bronwyn on the news, her auburn hair in a French twist, Chanel sunglasses, white linen suit, Italian sandals, looking unfamiliar, haughty and distant as she left the courts after Ari's arraignment. Inadvertently, he was sure, the mercenary woman he'd once believed he loved had married a crook; and now the crook's money was lost to her.

"I want to know what you think," Louisa repeated, "about how this will affect the ITRF election."

How what will affect it? Patrick didn't want to admit just how inattentive he'd been. Andrew Preston, the American candidate for the presidency of the International Thoroughbred Racing Federation, had publicly supported Louisa when she'd been arrested. His generosity had set the stage for a tentative but positive relationship between his family and hers, but Louisa still seemed to prefer media giant Jacko Bullock. Patrick couldn't share her predilection. The Bullocks, Jacko and his father, Mezner, were in the pocket of people like Ari Theodoros—or so Patrick believed.

A Toyota turned down the driveway, then stopped at the gatehouse. The guard spoke briefly with the driver before the truck continued its approach. It was ancient-looking—and sounding. A muffler would be a good idea. The driver was Vietnamese, Patrick thought, maybe one of Louisa's gardeners. He considered speaking to the man about getting the four-wheel drive fixed, and then he saw it draw to a stop outside the entrance to the kitchen. A woman with long, very straight auburn hair climbed out, followed by a boy in a soccer uniform, who promptly began playing with a soccer ball he'd brought with him, dribbling, popping it in the air, regaining control, until the redhead told him to stop.

"Perhaps if you looked at me, Patrick, you would hear what I'm saying."

"What?" He spun around.

His great-aunt turned sympathetic eyes upon him, an unusual move for Louisa, who was straitlaced and not given to sympathy for herself or anyone else. "Are you worried about Megan being with Dylan?"

"Of course not," he said, though that wasn't strictly true. Dylan had regarded Louisa as the chief suspect in Sam's murder, but he had also been the one to track down Sandy Sanford, the real killer. And he had to admit, in comparison to some of the men Megan had dated in the past, Dylan Hastings was a dream come true. And Dylan's teenage daughter seemed to add new dimensions to Megan's life; the two were quite a pair with their shared interest in art and fashion, among other things. "No, I'm sorry. I was thinking about this morning's news. I apologize."

"Aristotle Theodoros," Louisa said with a snap in her voice. "Lower than a snake's belly. I'm tired of hearing about the man."

"You've met him?" Louisa was a wealthy and powerful woman. It didn't surprise Patrick to learn she may have met Theodoros at some point.

"Well, of course," she replied irritably. "His television show sold racing predictions. I was not at all surprised to learn he was involved in doping horses. I'm glad someone finished him off. It will save the country the money that would have been spent prosecuting him."

"Do you think he was murdered," Patrick asked, "to keep him from telling what he knew?"

"Probably." She gave a small snort. "People like that just give the sport a bad name. I know it's a cliché to say so, but it's a fact. Then people think racing is populated by underworld characters. Or they think it's all about money. Some people don't understand what it is to love horses and to love to see them run, especially an animal who loves running, a great horse whose heart will spend itself to win, win, win. An Indecent Proposal, for instance. That's a horse. There's spiritual beauty in horseracing, Patrick, and then on the other side are people like Aristotle Theodoros. Parasites."

Patrick turned his mind firmly to matters of the present. "How can you be sure Jacko Bullock isn't one of those?"

"I can't be. But I trust him more than I do Andrew Preston."

"What do you have against Preston?" Patrick tried to keep his voice neutral.

Louisa's face tightened slightly. "I don't like change, Patrick. That's all. And I don't like situations I can't control."

Patrick agreed with the sentiment that Andrew Preston wasn't about to be controlled by anyone. His mind's eye, however, continued to see the long, straight auburn hair of the woman who'd gotten out of the Toyota, reminding him of another woman with long, straight auburn hair.

"Wesley," Bronwyn hissed at her son as she finally persuaded him to sit on a stone wall outside the head housekeeper's office. "I'm trying to get a job," she said, moving her full-size backpack—one that had belonged to Ari—and Wesley's smaller tote bag so that they sat together. Bringing everything she owned to Fairchild Acres hadn't been practical. Instead, she'd hired a small—very small—storage unit in Sydney and prayed that she'd find a way to pay the monthly rentals until she could collect the rest of her belongings, belongings for which she was pretty sure there would be no room in the Fairchild Acres employee bungalows.

"It's important that you are quiet and stay out of the way here," she continued whispering to her son. "I have to have this job. Don't you see that? We have no money since your— Anyhow, we have to make our own way, Wesley, and that means I have to work."

"Why couldn't you get a job in Sydney?"

"It's expensive to live in Sydney." This wasn't the whole reason for her calling about the job she'd seen advertised at Fairchild Acres, however, and Wesley seemed to know it.

He said, "You always think you're smarter than everyone else."

"What are you talking about?"

"Like Nam. You thought he couldn't understand English."

Bronwyn's cheeks burned anew. When she'd bade their driver farewell, he'd said in perfect English, "He must have caused you a lot of trouble."

Ari.

Well, that was one way of putting it.

Yes, it was easy to blush, remembering her mistake.

"Wesley, could you please sit here quietly while I go in for my interview?"

"What if you don't get hired?"

Bronwyn didn't want to think about that. "I'm going to get hired. Now stay here. Don't wander around."

She approached the door of the estate manager's office, which was labeled Office, as she'd been told it would be. She knocked, and as she did, a small, extremely pretty young woman with short blond hair looked out of the next door, which stood open. It appeared to be the door to the kitchens, though also part of the main house.

"She's not here," the woman called.

"What?" Bronwyn turned.

"Are you here about the dishwasher's job?" the blonde asked.

Bronwyn nodded, noting the perfection of her skin

and thinking that Patrick Stafford had no shortage of beautiful women at Fairchild Acres. But he probably had a girlfriend, for all Bronwyn knew. She certainly wasn't here to resume any romantic relationship with him after a ten-year separation. Nonetheless, this pretty female made Bronwyn want to find the nearest sink and mirror so she could clean up after the hot, dusty truck ride. How could anyone come out of that obviously steaming kitchen looking so good?

"Well, Mrs. Lipton is gone for the day. She'll be back tomorrow. You've come on her day off."

"But I have an appointment." This was impossible.

"You're the woman who's supposed to be coming tomorrow?" the blonde asked, her eyebrows drawing together.

How could there be such a mix-up? Bronwyn wondered. It was late in the afternoon and Nam had already headed back to Sydney. Not that she could have afforded to have him make the trip again the next day. Were there hotels nearby? Bronwyn wasn't destitute, but she didn't want to spend any of the little cash she possessed. She could live on the smell of an oily rag better than most, but there was no point in depleting her resources unnecessarily.

"Look, I'm Marie," said the blonde, sticking out her hand, which Bronwyn took, grateful for the offer of friendship which the woman seemed to be making.

"Bronwyn Davies."

"Yes, now what you want to do is go over to that door and go in and find Agnes. She's the assistant housekeeper, and I dare say she'll find you a place to sleep tonight. Is that your boy there?"

"Yes, that's Wesley."

Marie nodded, smiling. "He's a handsome one, isn't he?"

"Too handsome for his own good," Bronwyn admitted. "He's been known to get away with plenty." She hesitated. "Which door?"

Marie pointed, and Bronwyn turned to see where she'd indicated.

"Right. Well, thank you."

"No worries."

As Marie ducked in the kitchen, Wesley said, "Brilliant, Mum. Wrong day."

Bronwyn nodded in resignation. "Well, you better come with me." She stooped to shoulder her heavy pack then fastened the hip belt. Wesley picked up his tote, swinging the strap over his shoulder. Bulging with his most prized possessions, the bag seemed to dwarf him, and Bronwyn thought how very young he was to have to go through all that he had in the last months—culminating, of course, in Ari's murder.

I've got to stop saying nasty things about Ari, she thought.

After all, Wesley loved the man, loved his memory still.

Bronwyn, too, had loved Ari. Once.

I can't think about it, about any of it. Unlikely as it might have seemed that she had loved a man twenty years older than her, that had been the case. Probably her attraction to him had something to do with the fact she'd never known her own father, who'd died before she was born, leaving Bronwyn's mother to fend for herself and her infant in urban Sydney.

Bronwyn would do a better job of that than her mother had. She and Wesley were not going to do any sleeping under bridges—or in shelters, for that matter.

She said, "Wesley, you're the best, y'know?"

"Mmm," he answered.

She led the way up a red stone path to the door Marie had indicated. As she turned up the path, the door at the end opened, and a man stepped out.

Her breath caught, and she stumbled on the walk. Graceful, Bronwyn.

She would have known him anywhere, and already her eyes were seeking out that cleft chin, the jaw and delicate yet prominent bones she remembered in his face. His medium brown hair was a little too long, parted on the side, and still had a tendency to dash across his hazel eyes.

The eyes Wesley had inherited.

Patrick Stafford stopped in his tracks. He paused, gave her one derisive look, and said, "Why doesn't this surprise me?"

Chapter Two

Patrick Stafford wasn't surprised to see her? Well, Bronwyn wasn't surprised to see him, either. After all, wasn't seeing him part of her purpose in coming to Fairchild Acres? Hadn't she subtly quizzed college friends about the old crowd until they'd gotten around to Patrick, until finally she'd learned where he was? He was Wesley's father, and both father and son deserved the chance to meet, to get to know each other.

But now, face-to-face with Patrick, Bronwyn remembered how angry and hurt he'd been when she'd refused his proposal. *We were so young,* she thought. She definitely intended to let him know that Wesley was his son, but not in front of Wesley.

He paused, seeming to take in the heat, sweat, dirt, backpacks, soccer ball, everything.

"I'm looking for the assistant housekeeper," Bronwyn said.

"And here I was sure you were looking for me."

He had a fine nose, perfect for looking down at her, Bronwyn thought.

"Let me fill in the blanks," he added, "to save you the trouble."

He stood over her, and Bronwyn felt the weight of the burden on her hips and shoulders and wished she could set down the huge pack, but it was too much trouble to get it back on.

"Sugar daddy is gone," he said, "so you tracked down Patrick Stafford to see if he might step in."

The presumption floored Bronwyn. On top of the heat, the truck ride, the mix-up over the days, this was too much. Patrick thought she hoped he would support her? How ridiculous. "Even I," she said, "don't have such an inflated opinion of my own charms."

"Your arrival here on the tails of Theodoros's untimely demise strikes me as more than coincidental."

As it was. The job opening at Fairchild Acres had been pure serendipity, but Bronwyn had hunted job ads in the Hunter Valley in the hope of finding *something*. She was hanged if she'd admit so now, especially with Wesley listening.

"Do you mind?" she said, her eyes indicating that a

child was present, a child who regarded Aristotle Theodoros as his father. For the first time she wondered if maybe Wesley might be better off without Patrick in his life. How insensitive could the man be, talking so casually about Ari's "untimely demise"? "You could actually point us in the right direction. I have an appointment with Mrs. Lipton for tomorrow about a job in the kitchens. I thought it was today, and we've arrived too early."

"Then, you ought to trek out to the highway and get a lift to the nearest hotel."

After Marie's kindness, Patrick's callousness stung. Suddenly, Bronwyn felt close to breaking down. But she managed to repeat, "If you could let the housekeeper know I'm here or tell me where to find her."

Patrick saw that her lips, lovely lips against that honey-colored skin he remembered so well, trembled. *You ass, Patrick,* he thought. There wasn't a chance in the world that Bronwyn's showing up here was coincidence, but she had no chance of worming her way into his good graces. So why not behave decently toward her? She was, after all, a widow accompanied by a young child, and the kid didn't deserve to suffer for his mother's—not to mention father's—crimes.

The boy would be mourning the loss of his dad; that would be natural.

Turning, he nodded toward the door in the big house through which he'd just come. "Go on in. Agnes is inside, first door on the right." Then, looking again at the kid, whose gaze had now turned cold—toward him, Patrick realized—he sighed and pulled open the screen. "Come in. We have room for you for the night."

Bronwyn marveled that Patrick even smelled the same. It wasn't a strong scent, and she hadn't been terribly close to him, yet he smelled familiar, from that years-ago time when they were lovers, back when she'd been a waitress in the campus coffee shop and he one of those lucky students who didn't have to work his way through uni.

"Agnes, this is Bron Theodoros—"

"Bronwyn Davies," Bronwyn corrected. *Bron.* Many people naturally shortened her name to Bron. Ari had hated it. *Like "brawn." You're not brawny.* And Bronwyn had begun to insist upon the use of her whole name—even in the last weeks she'd retained friendship with Patrick before their horrible parting.

Patrick cast her a quick look, but didn't argue. "Bronwyn Davies and her son..."

"Wesley," Bronwyn supplied.

"Bronwyn has an appointment with Mrs. Lipton tomorrow, and she arrived on the wrong day. I'm sure we can put these two up for the night in the house." He put subtle emphasis on the last three words. "Bronwyn and I are old acquaintances from uni."

"If there's room in the employee cottage," Bronwyn put in, "I'm sure that will be fine."

"Well, the available room got painted out there, and I know it's no good tonight because of the fumes," Agnes told her. Agnes was a fiftyish woman who wore her hair in a neat French twist. Her black-and-white uniform was spotless. Bronwyn remembered that Marie, in the kitchens, had worn a T-shirt with Fairchild Acres on it, so Bronwyn supposed that would be her uniform in the future. "We can put you up in the western corner."

Hot, Bronwyn thought. But the house was air-conditioned, blessedly so, so even the west part would be lovely. A roof over her head would be terrific.

"Is the room ready?" Patrick asked.

"Certainly," said Agnes, with an air of being vaguely insulted at his suggestion that it might not be.

"Then I'll show them the way," he said, surprising Bronwyn again. Nonetheless, she couldn't believe that he was doing so as a gesture of hospitality. No doubt he planned to tell her again that he wasn't going to support her. As if she would let him. She'd only wanted to give him the chance to know Wesley. But now she'd begun to wonder if that was such a good idea.

She and Wesley followed Patrick down the hall to a stairway, which, though clearly not the main set of stairs, was wide and led to an upstairs open hallway that looked down on what appeared to be a conservatory below. The upstairs hall was lined with photographs of horses, horses covered with blankets of roses, horses in the winner's circle. Accompanying many of them was the same tall, straight-backed woman at different stages throughout her life. Bronwyn had seen her before—from a distance at one or two events she and Ari had attended—and in photographs, as well. Louisa Fairchild. Bronwyn half hoped she would never come face-to-face with the Hunter Valley matriarch. Would Louisa meet any prospective employee? Bronwyn could just imagine the reaction of this seemingly indomitable woman at the news that Aristotle Theodoros's widow was on the premises. Did she dare ask Patrick not to mention the fact?

No. He would scorn her for asking him to help her cover up for…for what?

For having been married to a criminal.

There were two upstairs bedrooms in the south corner, and they shared a bathroom. The actual corner room with its four-poster bed was to be Bronwyn's, and a smaller room looking out on one of the paddocks was Wesley's.

"No soccer inside, mate," Patrick told Wesley as he showed him into the room, which contained a silky oak double bed.

"He knows that," Bronwyn said. She felt like a grease spot, but however miserably hot and sweaty she looked—and Bronwyn was far less sensitive to this question than any other woman she knew—Patrick shouldn't be assuming that Wesley hadn't been raised right.

"No doubt," Patrick answered coolly, "but Louisa wouldn't like it, so I thought I'd err on the side of caution."

"In that case, thank you," murmured Bronwyn.

"There are towels in the bathroom. If there's anything you need, please ask Agnes. The staff eats in the dining room attached to the kitchens, and I'm sure you'll be welcome there," he continued. "Maybe Wesley would like to spruce himself up a bit first."

Wesley looked baffled by the suggestion, but Bronwyn read the undercurrent in the words. Patrick wanted to speak with her alone. "Wesley," she said, "we did have a hot sweaty trip, and I'm definitely going to take advantage of the shower. Why don't you run yourself a bath first?"

"Okay," said Wesley, eyeing his mother and Patrick suspiciously.

Patrick stepped out of Wesley's room, and Bronwyn followed, closing the door behind her.

He said, "Please come and join me in my study. It's just down the hall."

Bronwyn knew it would be churlish to argue, so she followed him, remembering the breadth of his shoulders beneath the chambray shirt he wore, admiring his long legs in cream moleskin pants. Yes, he looked affluent and secure, yet he was also stiff, remote, serious, quite different from the Patrick she remembered from school. Of course, that Patrick hadn't been serious enough for her. A history major who'd wanted to travel and to write. Nothing specific, of course, and no sign of a genuine enthusiasm for writing. Just impractical plans. And then he'd asked her to marry him. And that proposal had suddenly accentuated for her how immature he was, how unready for marriage. She'd broken up with him and soon met Ari. A whirlwind courtship and another proposal of marriage, this one from a more mature man.

Of course, Ari's proposal had seemed to come from a legitimate businessman, not a mobster.

When had she begun to suspect the truth about Ari, the indecent truth that the person he seemed to be with his family was not at all the person he was in his business dealings? She shut the door on the question, a question she'd spent too much time examining over the months since Ari's arrest.

Patrick's study was a large, comfortable room, the furniture polished cherry, with a desktop computer which looked as though it could communicate with a space station and a separate rolltop desk complete with a banker's lamp. Prominently displayed on the small desk was a photo of Patrick and his sister, Megan, whom Bronwyn easily recognized. She stepped over to examine the photo. Megan's sense of style, her comfort with fashion, was apparent even in the head-and-shoulders photo, simply from her choice of earrings. But what Bronwyn remembered was the kindness of her eyes, eyes very much the shape of Patrick's, and the mouth that had always been so quick to laugh.

But Bronwyn also remembered the slight chip she'd had on her own shoulder when she'd first gotten to know Patrick's sister, whose childhood had been the antithesis of Bronwyn's. Megan was the product of exclusive private girls' schools, an affluent upbringing. Bronwyn, in contrast, had always been a survivor. "How is she?" she asked.

Patrick paused at the side bar, where several bottles sat on a silver tray. "Great. She's met a very nice man, a detective, actually, with a fourteen-year-old daughter. A cocktail?"

Bronwyn hesitated, reluctant to accept so much as a glass of water from this man who had accused her of coming to Fairchild Acres in search of a new sugar daddy. But a drink was what she very much wanted right now. That and the shower she'd told Wesley she planned to take before dinner. "Thank you," she said.

"Cognac?" he asked.

Bronwyn had never tasted cognac in her life until Patrick had ordered her some one evening when they were out together. *It's not exactly in my budget,* she'd pointed out.

He'd said, *Maybe if you get used to the finer things, they'll find you.*

That was before Aristotle Theodoros had appeared on the scene, a rival, an older man who was attractive to Bronwyn as a suitor and also filled the role of the father she'd never had—or something like that.

"Thank you," she said again.

Two snifters. He handed Bronwyn hers, and their fingers brushed. He lifted his glass. "Around here," he said, "we usually drink to horses. So, to Louisa's hopeful for the Outback Classic—An Indecent Proposal."

Bronwyn slid her eyes sideways, her mouth twisting in near amusement, and lifted her glass. "As long as you realize that I'm not here to make one."

They both drank.

"Then why are you here?"

The question was spoken quietly, and Bronwyn found herself watching his lips, his mouth, and thinking how unchanged he was and yet how completely different. He remained a very attractive man—one who had once been madly in love with her. He had walked away without looking back after she'd told him she was marrying Ari— that is, he'd left the coffee shop where she was working, hurried out into the parking lot. She'd been horribly worried then, her stomach tensing up, and had hardly been able to finish her shift. She'd been afraid Patrick would simply go out of his mind, but that wasn't all.

Part of her had feared that she was making a terrible mistake, that she was letting go of something she'd never find again and that she was foolish to marry Ari, that she and Ari could never be together what she and Patrick might have been.

Now Patrick had asked why she'd come to Fairchild Acres. Now was the moment to tell him about Wesley.

But to do so suddenly seemed rash. Patrick was rich, powerful. She had nothing. What if he tried to take Wesley from her? It wasn't as though the possibility hadn't occurred to her before; but the old Patrick hadn't been the kind of person to do that. This new Patrick? She wasn't sure. She had no way of defending herself, and the widow of a mobster wouldn't look so great in the courts. "I came for the job," she said.

"Knowing I was here?"

"Yes," she admitted. "I knew you were here. But I'm here because I need the work. The government has seized Ari's assets. I must support Wesley."

She could tell from the look in his half-closed hazel eyes that he didn't think her story credible.

Well, too bad. If he wanted to cherish conceited notions that she fantasized about getting back together with him, so be it.

Patrick wished he could read minds. He would gladly open Bronwyn Davies's head and see what had really brought her to Fairchild Acres. Whatever she said—and, face it, she'd just admitted that she'd known she would find him there—he had to believe she'd come here looking for him.

"Then let's get a few things straight," he said.

Bronwyn buttoned her lip, knowing what was coming.

"You're not going to get any special treatment from me. And don't entertain dreams about you and me picking up where we left off. If you haven't acquired any new job skills since you worked in that coffee shop, it's time you developed some."

Bronwyn took a drink of cognac, wanting to tell him a few home truths but knowing that doing so might influence her ability to secure the job in the kitchens.

Instead she said, "Please believe that it's with the greatest reluctance I accepted the offer of sleeping in this house tonight, let alone enjoying this drink with you. I would be a fool if I believed any man whom I'd once rejected would come back for more."

"Ouch," Patrick murmured.

She shrugged. "I don't think you're giving me this charming lecture because you've forgotten I once decided to marry someone else."

Ouch again, he thought. But Patrick knew that her ability to stick up for herself, the integrity that had never made him think everything he did was perfect, were part of what had attracted him to her in the first place. The women he'd known before Bronwyn had all been afraid of losing his favor by being less than agreeable; they'd seemed to worship him. But Patrick hadn't wanted that. He'd wanted a partner, an equal.

And just now—well, she was probably being snotty because he was letting her know how things would be if they were both around Fairchild Acres. "Can you imagine my *not* being suspicious of your motives under the circumstances?"

"No," Bronwyn replied, but she wasn't about to relieve him of his suspicions. She decided to distract him. "What *did* bring you here, Patrick? As I recall, you weren't on the best terms with your great-aunt."

"We weren't on any terms with her, good or bad," he admitted. "But she invited Megan and me to Fairchild Acres, and I wanted to hear what she had to say. I have to admit, I've grown fond of her. And protective."

Bronwyn managed not to say that of course Patrick would be protective of Louisa Fairchild's money, especially if he hoped to inherit part of it.

Instead, she asked, "And what are you doing with yourself these days?" She knew the answer; the same friends who'd mentioned where he was had supplied that information.

"The stock market. Must be in the blood."

Bronwyn well remembered when he'd seemed allergic to the possibility of doing anything so practical.

He turned from where he stood by the bar, and Bronwyn felt him assessing her. She knew he was examining her clothing, her figure, her general appearance. The thing about growing up on the streets was that she'd become used to other people being her mirror. She'd also learned to base her feelings of self-worth on things other than her physical appearance. How she treated people, her competence in life, a whole host of things were more important. But Patrick was a cipher. She couldn't guess his reaction to anything about her. Except the suspicion that he hadn't needed to put into words.

"Should I express condolences?" he asked.

"That's entirely up to you. I'm a widow, and that's considered good manners." The callous way he'd spoken of Ari's death—more than once—upset her, but she wanted to make as few waves as possible. She finished her cognac then and said, "In any case, I think I'll go see if Wesley is done with his bath."

Wesley had filled the huge claw-foot tub with as much water as he would have used at home, the home they didn't have anymore in Sydney, the home they didn't have anymore in Greece, the home they didn't have anymore in Queensland, any of the homes that weren't theirs anymore.

Why had his mother brought him here? Why couldn't she have gotten a job in Sydney so that he could have stayed at his school?

Then he remembered the past few months, the friends who wouldn't come over anymore because of who his father had turned out to be, the friends whose houses he couldn't go to because his mother had found out things about their parents. All right, she'd managed to convince him that moving away from Sydney would make him happier in the long run. But it sure wasn't happening yet. The Hunter Valley was full of rich kids, too, he knew, and he was not a rich kid any longer; his mother had made that pretty clear.

And who was that man who had finally introduced himself as Patrick, a friend of his mother's from uni? Obviously, he didn't want them here, but his mother must have known Patrick would be here when she decided to come to Fairchild Acres.

He had to admit there were some very nice lawns here, perfect for kicking a soccer ball, but his mum had said he couldn't play on them till she found out if it was all right with the owner.

Yes, he was just going to be an employee's kid, and there weren't any other kids here that he could see. His life was horrible.

And his father was dead.

Did his mother hate his father because she'd found out he was a criminal? She'd become so brusque all of a sudden, always in a hurry, constantly issuing orders. She'd told him, *I'm just concentrating on surviving, Wesley. That's what we've got to think about now. Making sure we have a place to live.*

His father used to be free with money, but his mum never had been. She used to get mad if she came in his room and found change on the floor. *Don't you understand how important money is, Wesley? I hope you'll always have enough, but you need to treat it with respect.*

Did they have enough money now? His father had said his mother worried too much about money; she'd always have plenty. Well, now *he* was worried about money.

And his father was dead.

After a brief discussion with Wesley on the necessity of conserving water, especially in the country, Bronwyn left him occupied in his temporary bedroom, reading a manga comic book he had brought with him, and headed for the bathroom herself. There, she stood under the spray of the shower, praying, begging. Begging a divinity by any name to give her the job she'd come here to obtain.

But was getting this particular job so important anymore? Patrick had been so rude, so presumptuous, that the thought of telling him that Wesley was his son held no appeal whatsoever. Bronwyn knew men, understood them. Patrick's ego was obviously still smarting from her rejection of his proposal almost eleven years before. Bronwyn didn't flatter herself that any attraction remained on his side, but a man like Patrick... Yes, the bitterness would remain.

How would he treat Wesley, then? It wasn't beyond the realm of possibility that he would completely reject his son.

And what was all this stuff about her coming to get money from him? Did he think she was that devious? Or just insane? In any case, it offended her to be perceived as a gold digger. When had she ever not worked for a living? Even when she'd lived with Ari, she'd contributed to caring for all of his homes, working right alongside the staff whenever a dinner party or other entertainment was planned. Ari hadn't wanted her to hold an outside job, or even to finish her degree in sports nutrition and physiology, wanting her instead to manage his homes and devote herself to Wesley. And she'd thrown herself completely into the role of mother, volunteering at Wesley's school, going to soccer and rugby and cricket practices. Shutting off the water to soap her hair, Bronwyn wondered if being a mother counted as work to someone like Patrick Stafford.

Like Patrick?

What was Patrick actually like? He seemed so different, even dressed differently, from the way he had as a student. Now he was a stockbroker, and the wild, romantic dreamer was gone. Bronwyn knew that there was a steadiness and self-confidence to Patrick now that hadn't been there when he'd been fantasizing different futures for himself. But there was an aloofness and distance, too. And Bronwyn was curious. Because of Wesley.

But it wasn't because of Wesley that she noticed that Patrick was still a very attractive man, more attractive, if possible, than he had been at university.

Well, that was natural. There was probably even some biological reason for her being interested in Patrick that way, something to do with his being

Wesley's father. In any event, she wouldn't be seeing much of Patrick, once she started work in the kitchens.

If she was hired at all.

Patrick was not sleeping. He resented that he wasn't sleeping, that seeing Bronwyn should keep him awake. What was she up to anyway? Why had she come to Fairchild Acres, knowing he was there, to get a low-paying job in the kitchens? The answer had to be him. She denied wanting money from him, but Patrick wasn't sure he believed that. Did she want to take up where they'd left off? Crazy. But she was here for a reason. Everything Bronwyn did was deliberate. Coincidence did not stretch far enough to explain her winding up in the same place as him.

But the question troubling him was whether the puzzle of her being here was what was really keeping him awake. Or was it just Bronwyn? She was, if anything, more beautiful than before. It was easy to believe she'd been living in luxury for the past ten years. Her honey-colored skin showed no sign of age. And that hair, the long red hair, the green eyes, whose color struck so forcefully. Lying awake in the dark, he saw not a money-grubbing widow with schemes in her heart; he saw Bronwyn. Bronwyn, Bronwyn, the only woman who'd ever broken his heart. The only woman he'd truly loved.

Chapter Three

"My only trouble with giving you this job," said Mrs. Lipton the next day, "is that you're overqualified. I haven't had much luck keeping people from the city, let alone university-educated workers, here."

"I didn't finish," Bronwyn said, because this was an important distinction as far as she was concerned.

"Nonetheless. Well, we'll give it a try. We have a room in the employee bungalow for you and another for your son. Ordinarily he would have to share with the other children, but there are none living in the bungalow. Only a few of the staff actually live at Fairchild Acres. Most of them are local."

Bronwyn nodded. "Thank you very much. I'm glad for the chance to do this job."

The housekeeper, a middle-aged woman whose hair was neatly styled in a short cut, studied her. "Are you a horse lover?"

"Not especially," Bronwyn admitted. Then she realized her error.

Mrs. Lipton said, "What brought you from Sydney? I would think, with your background, you could have found a better job there."

Bronwyn was ready. She'd known this question would come up. "I wanted a change of scene for my son. I was searching for the kind of place where I wanted him to grow up and decided that the Hunter Valley looked perfect."

"But it's expensive to live here, dear, if you're looking to own your own home sometime."

Bronwyn tried again. "My husband died recently, and it was painful to remain in Sydney." That much was certainly true. Reading the housekeeper's sympathetic look, she decided this would be her main story from now on.

"Well, let's get you your Fairchild Acres shirts, and then I'll take you out to the kitchens. Or perhaps first we should settle your boy into the cottage."

"Thank you," Bronwyn said again.

Wesley was her worry now, Wesley with too much time on his hands while she was in the kitchens. The sooner she could register him in the local school the better.

"Lipton!"

The voice came from outside. The housekeeper stood up, and so did Bronwyn. They went outside, and Bronwyn hung back as an elderly woman in trousers and a button-down shirt said, "There is a dog in the kitchens. We can't have that. Not around the food preparation area. It's a stray, I think. It would be best if you could call someone to take it away."

Wesley, sitting on the stone wall outside the office, peered up at Bronwyn, and she gave him a small wave, but kept her attention on the figure who was giving instructions about a dog. This was Louisa Fairchild, and Bronwyn couldn't help staring. The woman radiated confidence and charisma, and Bronwyn could tell that Mrs. Lipton genuinely liked her employer. Bronwyn could think of no finer recommendation for a human being.

Louisa Fairchild glanced over at her. Mrs. Lipton said, "Bronwyn Davies, our new dishwasher. Bronwyn, this is Miss Fairchild."

Bronwyn tried hard to meet the older woman's eyes as Louisa gave her a curt nod, seeming preoccupied.

"The dog, Lipton," Louisa Fairchild repeated.

Bronwyn was glad to escape the matriarch's piercing gaze.

If only she never finds out who I am or that I was married to Ari.

Doping horses. Racing fraud. Damn it, Ari. Why didn't you think about Wesley and me, about what would happen to us if you were caught?

She blinked the thought away.

All her recollections of Ari were now tinged by what she hadn't known about him. Or *had* part of her known? No, not really, Bronwyn answered herself honestly. She'd assumed that not all his investments were politically correct, but she'd never believed he'd do something criminal.

Maybe you didn't want to know, Bronwyn.

If she hadn't loved him, all of it would be easier now. But she'd loved him all right. Fallen for him hard since he was the antithesis to Patrick's youthful romanticism. Ari was steady, responsible, so appreciative of her. She'd loved her life with him.

But now, how could she mourn a crook? Who would care that he was dead or that she missed any part of him? He'd left her so isolated. She hadn't maintained one friendship separate from her life with him. Couples. They'd known other couples, Ari's business associates. If these friends weren't implicated in Ari's fraud, they'd been hurt by association with him.

Yes, she'd needed to get out of Sydney, had even considered leaving the country, starting over where no one knew her, where no one would see her as a wife who'd turned a blind eye to her husband's criminal activities.

Marie dragged the animal in question out of the kitchens. He was just a puppy and looked half-starved.

Louisa Fairchild said, "Looks like a dingo to me."

Marie watched her employer with an apprehensive expression, then told the dog, "You stay out."

The puppy, who was gray with black spots, sat down and scratched one oversize black ear.

"Part heeler," Mrs. Lipton pronounced.

"Well, let's get him out of here."

"I can watch him and make sure he doesn't go back inside."

Bronwyn stared. It was Wesley who'd spoken. He had jumped up from the stone wall where he sat beside the baggage they'd lugged from the house. Today he wore his child-size Manchester United uniform, and it struck Bronwyn how small he was, how young, as he marched up to Louisa Fairchild. Bronwyn wanted to tell him to stop, to sit down again, but her mouth wouldn't work.

The elderly woman gazed at him as though she'd never seen a child before. "Where did he come from?" she asked Mrs. Lipton.

Bronwyn stepped forward, her hand on her throat.

The estate manager gave her a reassuring smile. "He's your son, isn't he, Bronwyn?"

"Wesley," Bronwyn supplied.

"Theodoros," said Wesley, too softly to be heard by anyone but his mother, who considered infanticide.

He went over to the puppy and crouched down beside it, and the dog licked its lips, sticking out his tongue, lifting his head.

"All right, Wesley," said Louisa Fairchild. "I'm Louisa. Your job is to keep that animal out of the kitchens. We'll see if we can find him something to eat. Welcome, Bronwyn," she finally said, and Bronwyn detected no sign of recognition in the other woman. "We're glad to have you."

As she hurried away, toward the big house, Bronwyn released a breath she hadn't realized she'd been holding. Louisa's attitude put to rest both her greatest fears, that she would be identified as Ari's widow and that Wesley would be in the way and unwelcome.

"Let's go see where we're going to be living, Wesley," she told him. "I guess you better bring the dog. You can keep him outside, though."

"There have been dogs in the employee quarters before," Mrs. Lipton said. "In fact, there's a Lab mix who considers himself part of the place. You'll meet him. His name is Sergeant."

Things were looking up, Wesley decided as his mother went off to her job. The puppy wasn't his, but he would get to look after him, because the big boss had told him to. Wesley decided to call him Beckham, and he played with him outside the house where he and his mother were now going to live.

Halfway through the afternoon, a blond woman he'd seen the day before strolled back to the bungalow. She stopped beside the steps, where Wesley sat, bored from watching the dog. "I'm Marie," she said. "Your mum already told me you're called Wesley."

"Yes."

"So it looks like this is your dog now. He's a nice little guy. What are you going to call him?"

Wesley told her.

She took in his soccer uniform and smiled. "Very appropriate. Well, let's see if we can find Beckham a collar. If you take him over to the stables, you can ask Mike, the head groom, if he has something that will work."

"Thank you," Wesley said, keeping in mind that he had to be polite so that his mother didn't lose her job.

Marie squinted at him. "You remind me of someone."

"My dad always said I looked like my mum."

He saw her face soften into a curious and sympathetic expression. "Are your parents divorced?"

"No, my dad died," Wesley said. His mother had instructed him not to tell anyone who his father was. Still, he couldn't help saying, "He was murdered."

Marie exclaimed, "Oh, I'm so sorry. I had no idea, Wesley. You must miss him."

Wesley nodded, glad that someone, at least, understood how he felt. Not that his mother didn't understand.

Just before he went to sleep last night, she'd said, "I know you miss him, and I'm sorry, Wesley. I know it hurts. I'm really sorry." But his mother was also preoccupied and worried, anxious about money. He liked this sympathetic stranger.

He patted Beckham, and the dog huddled against his legs.

Patrick didn't see Bronwyn in the morning. He imagined she'd gone to her job interview. He hoped she wouldn't be hired. He hadn't slept well. In fact, he wasn't sure he'd slept at all. Bronwyn was the reason. He didn't need some woman scheming around him, and her intentions, whatever they were, couldn't be good. It must be money she wanted, no matter what she said to the contrary. Nothing else made sense.

At the breakfast table, Louisa talked about An Indecent Proposal's recent win at Warrego Downs and about Jacko Bullock's upcoming campaign gala. She did not talk about the murder investigation or her relief that Dylan Hastings had finally found Sam Whittleson's true killer. Patrick knew his great-aunt had a gift for holding a grudge, but she held none against Dylan for suspecting her. After all, he'd helped save Fairchild Acres from a recent fire, and he loved Megan.

"Patrick, did you hear me?" she said.

"What?"

She barely suppressed a look of irritation. "If you're not going to bother listening, I won't bother talking."

"I'm sorry. I was preoccupied."

"I noticed."

He found himself smiling, feeling terribly fond of her. "I was marveling over your attitude toward Dylan. You've certainly managed to forgive and forget."

"Well—forgive, anyway," she said tartly. "I've spent too much time harboring grudges."

Patrick lifted an eyebrow. People who'd known Louisa longer than he had remarked on the way her recent illness seemed to have changed her.

"Why should I expend energy thinking about someone who has wronged me?" she demanded. "If it's past, it's past. Dwelling on it just makes me a prisoner."

This made sense to Patrick. So why should he expend energy thinking about Bronwyn Davies Theodoros? Because she'd jilted him and accepted another man's proposal of marriage just weeks later? She'd said, "I'm marrying Ari, Patrick. I couldn't marry you because you're still planning a future that's incompatible with marriage— marriage to me, anyhow. You and I have different priorities, different values. Ari's and mine are the same."

Their values, Bronwyn's and Ari's? Money, money, money. When he'd said that, Bronwyn had shot back with unforgettable words. *Wrong, Patrick. Ari is a grown-up. And I'm in love with him.*

"Patrick, did you hear me?"

"I'm sorry, Louisa."

"I said that Megan called this morning. She and Heidi are coming up today to ride, and Dylan is coming with them. Will you have time?"

"Time for what?"

"To get to know the man your sister plans to marry."

"I do know him."

"Megan wants the two of you to be friends."

Patrick made a quiet, inarticulate sound.

Louisa sighed.

"He's fine," Patrick said. "She can marry who she likes."

"You know that he thought I'd covered up for the man he believed murdered his brother. When they were both children."

"I do know it," Patrick agreed.

"I know that must have prejudiced him against me, but it's all in the past now. At least make an effort, Patrick. For Megan." Then, before he could reply, she changed the subject. "There's a stray dog around," Louisa said, "and I've encouraged the son of one of our employees—a new hire—to look after him. Though I suppose he'll be going to school. The boy, I mean."

Patrick felt the force of all his unreasonable prejudice against Bronwyn, and he wanted to warn Louisa to watch out for the woman's machinations. Yet he wasn't sure how to broach the subject. And how would Louisa react to having Ari Theodoros's widow at Fairchild Acres? Surely she wouldn't like it, and perhaps he had a duty to tell her who Bronwyn was. But it seemed unfair. Bronwyn certainly wasn't going to dope horses.

Or was she? Was that what had brought her to Fairchild Acres, some scheme cooked up with the help of her late husband's nefarious business associates? And had she chosen this venue because he, Patrick, was here and she hoped for more leniency? Surely her college boyfriend would never suspect her of doping—or otherwise harming—horses.

The possibility alarmed him. She'd applied for work in the kitchens, but wasn't that an ideal place from which to influence operations in the stables? If something happened to a horse, who would think to question the kitchen staff?

But Bronwyn, hurt an animal?

"About the new hire," he began, uncertain what he was going to tell Louisa.

His cell phone vibrated on his hip. He looked at it, recognized the number of a client, and excused himself from the table to take the call.

"Patrick," said the man, a Sydney attorney. He and his wife had recently engaged Patrick to help them with some investment decisions. That morning, during his usual initial look at the stock exchanges, he'd seen how well those choices had paid off. "You've done terrifically, mate. Do we sell now?"

"I don't think so. You're in a very solid market. Let's

sit on it and let things grow," Patrick replied. He knew that this client's satisfaction would become word-of-mouth advertising and that he himself would gain more clients because of it. Yet today, it was hard to feel satisfaction about that—or about his own wealth, which certainly would never rival the empire Ari Theodoros had commanded.

It was as though Bronwyn's arrival had changed everything, making Patrick question who he even was. It shouldn't have that effect. Wasn't it her rejection of him and his youthful dreams that had galvanized him into pursuing finance?

After Patrick concluded the call, he found Louisa had finished her breakfast and gone out somewhere, probably to the stables. The horses of Fairchild Acres were her lifeblood.

I can't imagine Bronwyn hurting an animal, Patrick told himself again. Surely life with Ari Theodoros couldn't have changed her that much. But if something happened to one of the horses at Fairchild Acres, and if Bronwyn turned out to be responsible...

He was borrowing trouble. But he also realized he was protecting Bronwyn from possible consequences of Louisa's learning that she was Ari's widow. She didn't deserve his protection.

I'm going to tell Louisa, he thought. Bronwyn wasn't cut from the same cloth as Ari, and Louisa would take his word on that.

* * *

"This should do for a collar," said Walt, one of the grooms. He had found a leather piece of bridle, complete with a buckle, which fitted Beckham and left some room to grow. "And I know we've got leads you can use. Let's see." He sorted through the older tack hanging on the wall and pulled out a blue nylon one. "See how this suits you, mate."

Wesley took the lead and fastened it onto the collar Walt had found him. "Thanks. It's perfect."

Beckham, however, obviously didn't know the first thing about walking on a leash. As Wesley tried to lead him out of the barn, he preferred to sniff the straw and everything he could find.

"That's a sign," Walt said, "that he probably needs to go outside."

"Yes." Wesley managed to drag the puppy out of the barn. Then Beckham sat down in the dirt and scratched himself.

Louisa Fairchild walked toward Wesley, making her quick, precise way. "It looks like he's all set now," she said.

"His name's Beckham."

"That's an interesting name."

"For David Beckham, the soccer player."

"I don't know much about soccer."

Wesley expected the older lady to move off. She wouldn't be interested in the things he was.

But she said, "Do you like horses, Wesley?"

"I haven't been around them much. My dad—"
Abruptly he remembered that he wasn't supposed to
talk about his father. But that seemed so silly. Wesley
knew that his father hadn't drugged any horses himself.
He knew this because he read the papers, though his
mother had tried to keep them out of sight. He used to
find and take them from the garage and take them to his
room.

"Yes?" Louisa Fairchild arched her eyebrows.

"He knew about horses," Wesley decided to say.

"Where is your father?"

"He died."

The look of sympathy the old lady gave him made
Wesley feel warm inside, and suddenly he felt tears come
to his eyes. He turned away so that she wouldn't see.

"I'm so sorry," she said. "Perhaps you'd like to learn
about horses, too. You can remember your father that
way, by doing something which interested him. You can
be like him. Our loved ones, after they die, live on in us."

You can be like him.

Wesley wasn't sure he wanted to be like his father.
Once, he would have said that, yes, he wanted to be just
like him. But everything had gotten confused when his
father went to jail. It didn't seem okay to want to be like
him, because he had stolen people's money, basically,
or cheated them out of it. Just regular people, too, not
especially bad people. Just…anyone.

His mother had said once, "He was weak, Wesley."

Weak? Or bad? He'd asked his mother, and she'd said, "The hell of it is, I don't know and I can't tell you. Only your father could answer that question."

But, in any case, the old lady was being nice, and maybe she was one of those lonely old people his mother sometimes talked about, people with no one left who loved them.

So he said, "I'd like to learn about horses."

"I've just got to lose some weight," said Helena, one of the prep cooks, as she chopped carrots by the sink where Bronwyn was washing dishes.

Helena was more than heavy, Bronwyn could see, with almost three chins. Pity stirred in her heart, along with an old urge—it felt very old, pre-Ari—to do something to help. It was, in fact, the desire to help obese people that had led Bronwyn to study sports nutrition and physiology at university. She had done this because her own mother had been obese. Not back when they'd been homeless and living on the streets. Later, when, because of Bronwyn's first job, they were finally safe. Suddenly, her mother had experienced a weight gain of almost a hundred pounds, then diabetes and health struggles and sudden death.

Bronwyn had vowed to always stay in good shape herself. But she'd really wanted to do something for other people like her mother.

"I wasn't always like this," Helena volunteered. "I used to be closer to your size."

Bronwyn eyed the diet soft drink at Helena's elbow and said, "You might try drinking some juice instead of those."

"But the calories!"

"The thing is, if you eat something with nutritional content you'll probably be less hungry. In fact," she added, "studies have linked diet soft drinks with weight gain. They seem to make people crave more calories."

"You think? I sure wish I could lose weight. But every time I diet, I just end up putting it right back on."

"For me, anyhow," Bronwyn said, "nutritious food makes me feel better than things that are bad for me. So I'd rather have fresh fruit or vegetables or whole grains than things that have a lot of nonfood junk in them."

"You might be right about that."

"She's right!" chimed in Howard, the sous-chef. "You eat too many crackers, Helena."

"But they're low fat!"

"And there's nothing in them," he told her. "No nutritional value."

"I bet you work out, too," Helena said to Bronwyn.

"Not now. Back when I was married—" Bronwyn stopped abruptly.

"Wesley told me your husband died," said a woman's voice beside her.

Bronwyn started, but it was just Marie, sticking her hands beneath the tap to wash them.

"Oh, you poor thing," said Helena. "How did that happen?"

Omitting to tell her employer that she was Ari Theodoros's widow was one thing. But she didn't want to lie to coworkers, to people Bronwyn hoped would become her friends. After all, both Marie and Helena lived in the employee cottage where Wesley and Bronwyn would be staying. So Bronwyn said quietly, "He was murdered."

"Oh, God. I'm so sorry I asked you about it!" Helena exclaimed. "How terrible for you. But you don't have to talk about it anymore."

They were probably curious—Australia had few murders—but no one asked more.

Howard changed the subject. "You know, I think we should have an exercise class here, for employees. Do some yoga or something."

Howard was American. Besides working in the kitchen he was apprenticing to a local farrier. Louisa had a large kitchen staff for the size of her business, but Helena had explained that she did a fair amount of entertaining.

Marie asked, "Where could we have a yoga class, and when?"

"Before work in the morning or after we finish up at night," Howard suggested. "I bet Louisa would find some place for us."

"Yeah, you ask her," François, the chef, suggested, with the air of baiting him.

"All right, I will."

"But who's qualified to teach something like that?" Helena asked.

Bronwyn hesitated. Her leisure activities, while married to Ari, had been Iyengar yoga and running, things she'd done at university as part of her own physical fitness regimen. She'd also played on several teams at university and had volunteered coaching a girls' hockey team. She certainly had a strong sports background, and the course of study she'd pursued at school made her better qualified than most.

"I suppose I could," she said.

"I think Louisa has been surprised by what a fine horsewoman Megan is," Dylan Hastings told Patrick as the two men sat on Louisa's veranda late that afternoon.

"She ought to be good," Patrick replied. "She's been riding all her life."

The topic petered out, and Dylan raised his beer bottle to his lips again.

"I don't suppose, in your line of work," Patrick said, "You could check out someone's criminal background."

"It would depend on who—and why. What's on your mind?"

"Jacko Bullock. Louisa's supporting him for the ITRF presidency, and I'd hate to see her reputation suffer because of the guy."

"He's beyond my reach," Dylan replied. "He and his father are pros when it comes to self-protection. I doubt anything will come up in a routine check. What do you suspect him of?"

"Potential ties to organized crime. The members of the ITRF need to know who they're voting for. Louisa, for one, would never vote for a candidate she knew had links to organized crime."

"Well, you're not the first person to suggest it," Dylan agreed.

Patrick's eyes caught movement on one of the lanes that wound between the big house and the employee bungalow. It was Bronwyn's son, kicking his soccer ball. Kicking it back to his mother. He appeared to be attempting to score a goal between two trees beside the bungalow. Bronwyn was doing an admirable job defending the goal. A small dog sat nearby, sometimes running out to chase the ball.

"Who's that?" Dylan asked.

"A new employee and her son."

"Ah."

"Kitchen help," Patrick added, as though this was important. "Actually, I knew her at university. Old girlfriend. A little odd, her showing up here. To be honest, I don't like it."

Dylan said nothing to relieve his suspicion.

"She says she knew I was here." Patrick felt the renewal of all that morning's doubts—and some guilt that he hadn't yet told Louisa just whom she was harboring. Well, he wouldn't tell Dylan before mentioning it to Louisa.

"Think she wants to get back together?" Dylan asked.

"She claims to need a job. She was married to a wealthy man, but he died and his money went elsewhere."

"Unusual."

"Yes. I wouldn't have let it happen," Patrick couldn't stop himself from saying.

"That sounds protective."

"Of her?" Patrick snorted. "This woman can take care of herself, believe me. Well, maybe not financially. Or at least not in the style to which she has been accustomed." He knew he was being unfair to Bronwyn. After all, she'd worked while she was at university, and before that she'd lived in poverty. She was a survivor.

"It's hard being a single parent," said Dylan.

He would know, Patrick reflected. Dylan had been raising his daughter single-handed when Megan met him. And he hadn't done a bad job of it. Heidi was her own person, neither spoiled nor stifled.

"Does she have a degree?" Dylan asked.

Patrick didn't like to admit he'd gotten a look at Bronwyn's application—half to see the sight of her handwriting, fundamentally unchanged in ten years. "No. She didn't finish."

"What did she study?"

"Sports Nutrition and Physiology. As I recall, she wanted to help people build self-confidence by getting into shape. But I'm sure she has changed since then."

Dylan's eyes slid in his direction, but the cop said nothing.

Briefly, Patrick considered confiding more of Bronwyn's background to Dylan. Then, another thought occurred to him. If Megan saw Bronwyn and recognized her, Louisa would definitely find out Bronwyn had been married to Ari. Megan had been far more forgiving of Bronwyn's defection than Patrick had; still, his sister would want to protect family—him and Louisa.

The soccer ball flew toward the foot of the veranda, and the boy, Wesley, ran after it, followed by the puppy.

Dylan got up to jump down from the veranda and retrieve the ball. Patrick didn't know how he himself came out of his chair and off the veranda first, his foot passing the ball back to the boy.

Wesley said, "Will you guys play with us? Then we'll have four."

"Sure," Dylan answered, and introduced himself to Wesley.

Patrick's eyes met Bronwyn's across the lawn, the stretch of green so recently saved from fire. What surprised Patrick was that Bronwyn looked as displeased with her son's suggestion as Patrick felt.

Chapter Four

"Are you good?" Wesley asked Dylan frankly.

"I was a footballer. But I can run." Dylan turned and seemed to size up Patrick.

Wesley considered. He didn't want to be on Patrick Stafford's team, but he also didn't want Patrick on his mother's team. He might be mean to her. But before Wesley could choose, Patrick himself said, "Let's try you and me against Dylan and your mum, mate."

Wesley agreed. They began playing, and soon both men had their shirts off. Patrick was pretty good, which surprised Wesley. He began to think his mother and Dylan would be outmatched.

* * *

Bronwyn slid her foot out to steal the ball from Patrick and pass it to Dylan. She didn't intend to trip Patrick and certainly didn't mean to fall herself. Suddenly she was down on the still-smoky-smelling grass, and Patrick was sprawled half-across her, saying, "Are you all right, Bronwyn?"

"I'm fine." Why did he affect her this way after so long? Why did hearing him say her name start her pulse jumping in her throat? She glanced over and saw the familiar chin with that dent in it, the cheekbones as pronounced as Viggo Mortensen's, everything about Patrick so damned handsome. And he was in good shape still. She made herself look at her watch. "But I'm due back in the kitchen to help with dinner preparations."

"I thought you were a dishwasher."

"Yes, well, they're finding other uses for me."

Patrick stood up, then spontaneously offered her his hand.

She pretended not to see it, but got up on her own.

His irritation began to simmer anew.

Dylan was talking with Wesley about the dog.

Patrick said, "Nothing better go wrong while you're here, Bronwyn. I think you know the kind of thing I mean."

She spun, very white. "Actually, I don't."

"Problems with the horses."

Her mouth fell partway open, her eyes wide. Then, she turned and strode across the lawn without another word.

He had to tell Louisa—before Megan did and gave Louisa reason to doubt his loyalty. He didn't want to bring the subject up at the dinner table, so he sought out his great-aunt beforehand. Dylan, Megan and Heidi, although invited to dinner, had headed home. They planned to have some family time before Heidi returned to her new boarding school in Sydney, the same school Megan had attended.

Patrick found Louisa in the barn, talking to one of the grooms about An Indecent Proposal and how he'd done on the morning gallops. Patrick walked through the barn, checking on his own riding horse and re-membering the times in college when he'd invited Bronwyn out to his parents' place—recently become his through their deaths—when they'd ridden the family horses along the beach. Bronwyn had been a novice rider but a natural athlete and had actually taken some riding lessons subsequently, as part of her work on her degree.

"Were you looking for me?"

Patrick turned to see Louisa glance past him at Second Chance, his horse, a sorrel with a white star.

"Yes," he said. He spoke in a rush, the way he used to with his parents when he'd had to admit something he knew wouldn't make them happy—a dent in a fender, forgetting a chore, less than a top mark in school. "It's about your new hire, Bronwyn Davies."

"You started to say something this morning."

Not for the first time, Patrick marveled at Louisa's sharpness, which hadn't been affected by her recent heart problems. Though now she brought a cane with her when walking, he noticed that she used it less as a physical prop than a stage prop. "She's Ari Theodoros's widow." As soon as he said it, he remembered Louisa's heart condition and feared that the news would be too much of a shock.

"Actually, I know that."

"What?" He stared at her.

"I've seen her at functions over the years. And Megan has mentioned that Bronwyn threw you over for Ari years ago. Well, I hope you're not holding that against her, Patrick. Childish in someone your age."

He felt a head shorter. How had Louisa known all this? "Megan told you…when?"

"Weeks ago. We were discussing your bachelor status, your doubts about Dylan, all of that. It came up, and she meant no harm by it. She just said she thought you had something against women because of it."

"Oh, she did, did she?"

"I said that I gave you credit for greater maturity than to let the rejection of one woman sour you on the entire sex."

"Good. Because it hasn't." He'd dated over the years, had a couple of serious girlfriends. No one he'd wanted to marry. But one thing he knew for sure. If he ever did ask another woman to marry him, he would be certain of her answer first. Nonetheless, he didn't appreciate Louisa's turning his decision to warn her about Bronwyn into a chance to admonish him for supposedly never getting over her. He asked, "Don't you think it a little odd, though, that she should show up here now? She says she knew I was here."

"Did she?" Louisa seemed only barely interested. "I like her boy. You know, you'd be doing us all a favor if you'd take him riding with you sometime."

"Can he ride?" The suggestion had startled Patrick, so he stalled with a question.

"Well, he has to start somewhere, and I imagine you'd be a competent person to accompany him. Let him ride Meadow Boy." Meadow Boy was a twenty-two-year-old dressage horse, mellow, gentle.

"You think I have so much time on my hands that I should become a child-minder?"

Louisa glared up at him, and Patrick felt himself shrink again. "I think that you're the kind of man who has time for a grieving, fatherless boy who is probably desperately in need of a positive male role model."

"Do you have an ulterior motive here, Louisa?"

"Such as?"

"Encouraging me to tilt a lance at Bronwyn once again."

Louisa snorted. "You think I have so much time on my hands that I've become a matchmaker? Your love life is no concern of mine, Patrick, as long as it has no negative impact on Fairchild Acres. But I like Wesley Theodoros, and I think there are few things on this earth as important as the raising of children."

It was a surprisingly impassioned speech from Louisa. Of course, he'd also seen his great-aunt passionate on the subject of Dylan's daughter, Heidi. She did care about children. He just tended to forget it, because she cared so much about horses.

"So," he asked, "is this in the nature of an order?"

The older woman seemed to measure him with her eyes. "It's in the nature of an expectation." And without another word, she turned and started out of the barn, leaning on her cane.

Stage prop, Patrick thought.

Bronwyn liked working in the kitchens. Marie, Helena and Howard had all welcomed her as a friend, and they'd begun a morning exercise class in the living room of the bungalow. None of them had yet had the courage to ask Louisa for a place for their class, though Howard and Helena both thought she might be accommodating.

On her fourth evening at Fairchild Acres, after putting Wesley to bed with Beckham sleeping on the floor at his feet, she sat out on the cottage's veranda doing math. How much money could she save? How quickly? How long could she stay at Fairchild Acres? Would she ever be able to afford another home for herself and her son? Was there any chance she could finish school, earn her degree?

The numbers in her mind kept her thoughts off two subjects.

One: did she dare do as she'd intended in coming to Fairchild Acres and tell Patrick Stafford that Wesley was his son? She'd remembered Patrick as fun and light-hearted, but there was a new acerbity in his treatment of her; if he had an old score to settle, she couldn't let Wesley become a pawn in that game.

And Subject Number Two: Ari.

Bronwyn had loved him, had been in love with him, and when she'd learned the truth about his criminal activity, eight weeks ago at his arrest, she'd felt like a boat cast adrift with no rudder and no sail. Her world had become completely disordered as the things she'd believed proved false.

So she added up her future wages and looked forward to the following day, her day off, when she would go register Wesley at the local school. That couldn't happen soon enough, because Wesley had said today that Louisa Fairchild wanted him to have riding lessons and planned to ask Patrick to teach him!

That thought made Bronwyn's head spin.

A sound startled her, and she looked up into the darkness to see a tall, familiar shape passing on the lawn, carrying a shovel. Patrick wore work clothes and seemed to have been doing something in one of the pastures. He saw her, stopped, stared for a minute, then walked toward the porch.

"Still here," he said.

"Yes." The safest reply.

"Hard work is good for you. You can see how the other half lives."

Bronwyn couldn't stay silent. "I've never forgotten." *Patrick dear.* "If you'll remember, I was waiting tables while you were flitting to and from classes on the Napoleonic Wars and Ancient Greece and drinking beer in pubs in your free time." *I didn't say that. I didn't say that to Louisa Fairchild's great-nephew.* What if her loss of self-control cost her this job? She needed the job. "Look, I'm sorry, Patrick. It's been a long day. Please forget I said that."

He looked as though he required more than an apology.

"Obviously, you've become very practical and industrious," she added. "So I guess my turning you down all those years ago worked out for the best for you."

"Meaning?"

She had meant that perhaps her rejection had taught

him the value of a day job. "You seem content," she said, and hoped he would let the subject rest.

"Well, it did work out well for me." He leaned on the shovel and studied her. "I discovered what I really want in a woman."

Inside the bungalow, one of the dogs growled. It sounded like Beckham, but Bronwyn hardly registered it, so intent was she upon Patrick's words. "And what is that?" she asked.

"Someone independent, who isn't looking to me for her next meal."

"I've already said that's not—"

A scream from inside cut short her words. Wesley. She was out of the chair and running, and heavy footsteps pounded behind her. Through the living room cleared of furniture, past the now-growling Lab mix, past Marie's and Helena's doors banging open, and into Wesley's room, where she froze.

The light on the dresser was on, and Wesley stood on top of the dresser. On the ground Beckham barked and growled at a large brown snake.

All she could think was, *Don't bite the dog!*

Because the snake's focus was on the puppy, whose teeth were bared.

Behind her, Helena screamed.

One swift movement, a tall shadow looming beside Bronwyn, and the snake lay in two pieces.

"Oh, God," gasped Bronwyn, sagging against the

body beside her. Patrick had dispatched the snake with the shovel.

At her shoulder, Marie echoed her words.

Bronwyn swiftly shrugged away from Patrick as Wesley gamely leaped off the dresser and onto the floor. He hugged his dog, who had sat down and begun absently licking himself. "Brave boy, Beckham. He didn't bite Beckham, Mum, but Beckham was going to bite him."

Patrick picked up the long section of the snake, scooped up the head with the shovel, and carried both out of the room. Bronwyn sank onto her son's bed, trembling. *Don't bite the dog,* had been the beginning and the end in denial. *Don't bite my son. Don't kill my precious son.*

"Oh, God," she said again, touching Wesley's head as Patrick reappeared. Marie and Helena, after making sure no one had been hurt, returned to their own bedrooms.

"Yes, Beckham's as brave as Rikki-Tikki-Tavi," Patrick said.

"Who's that?" Wesley asked, staring blankly at the spot where the snake had been.

"You haven't heard of Rikki-Tikki-Tavi?" Patrick said. "That was my favorite story growing up. I've always been terrified of snakes." He didn't add that a snake had killed one of his dogs when he was growing up. He hated snakes, and when he'd cut this one in two with the shovel, sparing Wesley and Beckham, it had also been a stroke for his old Labrador, Snow. "Rikki-Tikki-Tavi was a mongoose in India."

"What's a mongoose?" Wesley asked. He climbed back up into his bed and patted the mattress beside him. Beckham jumped up and joined him.

Bronwyn gave her son a look, and Wesley deliberately ignored her. Beckham was not allowed on the bed. But how could she push him off after his bravery?

As though reading her mind, Wesley said, "Mum, he told me the snake was here. He growled, and then I turned on the light, and I climbed up as high as I could to get away from it. I was going to pick up Beckham, too, but I was afraid."

Thank God you were, Bronwyn thought.

"You were smart is what you were," Patrick said.

Warmth rushed through Bronwyn as he complimented her son. *Their* son. How good it would be for Wesley to hear that kind of praise from a man he knew to be his father.

But Wesley still believed Ari Theodoros was his father.

Overwhelmed by the situation in which she'd placed herself, Bronwyn remained silent.

"What's a mongoose?" Wesley repeated.

"If you like, tomorrow we can go up to the big house and get on the computer and look it up. I want to say that they're related to weasels or ferrets or both, but I could be wrong," Patrick told him. "In any case, they are extremely efficient at killing snakes."

Bronwyn wasn't sure she'd ever heard Ari utter the words *I could be wrong*.

"Would you like to hear about Rikki-Tikki-Tavi?" Patrick asked.

"Yes," Wesley answered. He got under his covers and lay back contentedly with his head on his pillow. "Do you know about him?" he asked Bronwyn.

"Yes," Bronwyn answered. "But I don't remember the story perfectly."

"Neither do I," said Patrick, "but I'll give it a go."

He drew out the desk chair and pulled it up beside Wesley's bed. "The story of Rikki-Tikki-Tavi was written by a man named Rudyard Kipling."

"The Jungle Book!" said Wesley.

"Very good. Well, Rikki-Tikki was a mongoose, as I said, and he lived in India."

Bronwyn was impressed with Patrick's storytelling. She curled up at the end of Wesley's bed and listened to Patrick describe Nag and Nagaina and the birds in the garden. The snakes hissed when they spoke and when they moved, and Rikki-Tikki-Tavi chattered and capered and cuddled with the boy whose life he finally saved.

She couldn't help enjoying the warm depth of Patrick's voice. She remembered that voice, remembered the feeling it had always given her. Well, when it wasn't saying things like, *I'm not sure what I'll do later on…maybe try and write a novel.*

He'd been so impractical! But obviously, he'd gotten over that, was no longer a footloose dreamer with vague plans for the future.

When the story ended, Wesley said, "I want to see what a mongoose looks like. Why aren't there mongooses in Australia?"

"Because they can wipe out all the snakes, which can lead to rodent overpopulation, among other things. But, believe me, I spent a good part of my childhood wondering the same thing." He gave a deliberate shudder. "I hate snakes."

"You nailed that snake. He was *big*," Wesley said, now seeming to delight in remembering the terrifying incident. "Was it a taipan?" he asked tremulously.

Patrick shook his head. "Too far south. It was an Eastern brown snake."

As if that's better. The taipan's reputation was nearly matched by that of this bad-tempered, venomous reptile. "I sincerely hope there aren't more of those around," Bronwyn said, then regretted saying it in front of Wesley.

"It's definitely the only one I've seen or heard about since I've been here," Patrick said. "You know we just had a big fire. It's possible that the fire drove the snake out of its usual habitat."

"Then more of them might have come out, too," Wesley said in a quiet voice.

"I'll have a good look around, shall I?" Patrick suggested.

"Yes, please…sir," Wesley added.

"And Louisa has said I'm to ask you if you would like to ride horses tomorrow."

"That's very generous of her," Bronwyn said. "But I'm going to register Wesley for school tomorrow."

"Surely that won't take all day. And how will you be getting into town?"

Bronwyn had already asked the other kitchen workers what they recommended. They said it would be best to catch a ride with one of the farm utes when someone was heading out on an errand. She told Patrick this.

"That could mean waiting around all day," he said. "I'll tell you what. I'll take the two of you at, say, nine. Then, when we're done, Wesley and I can go riding."

Bronwyn was unsure how to interpret his sudden interest in her son—*our* son, she reminded herself. Less than an hour earlier he had spoken bitterly of the lesson he supposedly had learned from her rejection of him; he'd said he'd learned the kind of woman he wanted. He'd also made it clear that she was not that woman. Bronwyn couldn't really believe that he thought she expected a handout from him after all this time. Undoubtedly, he'd suggested it to wound and insult her.

But now he seemed friendly toward Wesley, taking her son at face value. Well, Wesley was a likable child.

Bronwyn tucked him in bed once again and said, "If you're scared, come and get me."

Far be it from Wesley to admit fear in front of Patrick Stafford. "I'm not," he said.

Patrick stepped out of the room ahead of Bronwyn, who paused to turn out the light.

In the hall, Bronwyn noticed that the doors to Marie's and Helena's rooms were closed. Patrick said quietly, "Are *you* scared, Bronwyn?"

"Yes. At least I've got faith in these dogs, though." She paused to pet Sergeant, the estate's Lab mix. "You're a good boy," she told him. "You keep a watch out."

She found herself admitting to Patrick that her focus initially had been on Beckham, hoping the snake wouldn't bite the puppy. "I guess I was too terrified to admit it could get Wesley."

"Makes sense to me," he said and gave another shudder.

"You really don't like snakes, do you?" Bronwyn said.

"No. A brown snake killed my dog when I was a child."

"You never told me that."

"It's not my favorite topic. Like you, I'm glad Beckham is safe. Not to mention Wesley." In the darkened living room, where no one had yet bothered to turn on a light, he said, "I apologize for implying again that you came here looking for a handout. But I'd like to know why you *are* here, Bronwyn."

Could she risk it? Had the time come to tell him the

truth? She'd almost concluded that it had, but she wasn't willing to discuss it within earshot of Wesley. "I want to tell you," she finally admitted, "but this isn't the best time. Do you mind waiting till—" *Till what?* "This is turning out to be a good opportunity for me," she said instead. "Actually, the chef is interested in my background in sports nutrition. Marie and I had some good ideas about dishes which would help Louisa heal from her recent heart trouble. I hope she likes the food," Bronwyn continued, to fill any silence in which Patrick could ask again what she was really doing at Fairchild Acres. "And we're having an informal employee exercise class, too, which is fun."

Knowing that it was well past time to get out of Bronwyn's company, especially here in the dark bungalow, Patrick nonetheless said, "You never finished your degree, did you?" He knew the answer, but wanted to hear Bronwyn's feelings about her failure to get a university degree.

"I know. I would have liked to, but Ari thought it was unnecessary." To Bronwyn, the remark seemed disloyal, and then she wondered why she felt any loyalty toward Ari at all. Ari, whom she would never again see. Ari, who had been her husband and lover.

"You're grieving?" Patrick asked.

"I don't think about it. I never knew about—oh, the doping of horses, the betting shops, the illegal things— not until he was caught. At first I didn't believe it. Then,

I felt stupid. But he was a human being, not a monster. Which means I can't just decide to hate everything about him. Because I did love him. Except he wasn't the person I thought he was, so was it really him I loved?"

Patrick was unexpectedly touched that she was making these revelations to him. They reminded him of the old Bronwyn, who had always seen the world and the people in it as infinitely complicated, with a wide array of motivations for their behaviors. And, he felt that she was speaking to him as she would to a friend, and that touched him, too. Though he'd always spoken easily with Megan, it was rare in his experience for a woman to try to be a good friend to him. Most women seemed so intent on marrying him that they wouldn't tell him their real thoughts, perhaps for fear that he wouldn't like them. Bronwyn had never been like that. She'd always seemed to know who she was and been unafraid of being that person.

Past time to get out of here, he thought. Friendship was one thing. Befriending Wesley as a courtesy to Louisa was fine. Wesley's courage with the snake had impressed Patrick. And he was polite. Bronwyn had done a good job.

But he should be careful about spending too much time with Bronwyn…. He'd already volunteered to take her and Wesley down to the school the next day. It didn't help that she remained, for him, the epitome of feminine beauty. Everything about her was classic. Even now, in the shadows of the living room, he could make out the perfect curve of her chin and jaw, the line of her straight, slim nose.

He turned abruptly toward the door. "Well, good night." He strode out and did not look back. If he had stayed a moment longer, he might have touched her. And as he walked across the lawn toward the big house, he remembered the moment after he'd killed the snake, when Bronwyn had sagged against him.

And then she'd seemed to remember who he was and moved away.

Interesting how neatly she'd sidetracked discussion of what had brought her to Fairchild Acres. Well, the story would undoubtedly be interesting, but he wasn't going to beg her for it. And part of him still believed that it was going to be a request for financial support, in one form or other.

Chapter Five

Over the next few days, Patrick fell into a routine with Wesley. The boy had started at the local school and was riding the bus each way. Around four o'clock each day, Patrick wandered over to the bungalow and usually found Wesley finishing an afternoon snack. Then, Patrick and he would head for the barn to saddle Second Chance and Meadow Boy.

Every encounter with Bronwyn's son impressed Patrick more. Wesley was a remarkable child, easy-going, compliant and extremely pleasant to be around. And Patrick couldn't help but see, from her interactions with him, that Bronwyn had a lot to do with the way Wesley was turning out.

The boy was a natural athlete, and took to riding easily. Patrick soon considered taking him into town to look for some riding boots. But in the meantime, Wesley wore his Nikes.

On the first Friday after Wesley started school, as he and Patrick were riding around Lake Dingo to check on some of the stock, as Patrick had promised Louisa he would, Wesley said, "How do people dope racehorses?"

Alarm bells went off for Patrick. All his initial suspicion of Bronwyn rushed to the forefront of his mind. Then, it occurred to him that maybe Wesley was simply curious about what his father had done. "I don't know exactly," Patrick replied. "A veterinarian could better answer that question. But why do you ask?"

"Just wondered," Wesley said.

Patrick glanced over at him and saw that beneath the brim of his hat, Wesley was flushed.

"Are you asking because of your father?" He was going out on a limb here. What if Wesley didn't know about his father's convictions?

"How do *you* know?" Wesley said, gaping at him. "You don't know who my father is."

"Actually, I do, and so does Miss Louisa."

"But Mum said you all weren't to know, that then you'd think we were going to dope horses, too."

It was Patrick's turn to blush. Because, of course, he *had* wondered. But that was when Bronwyn first arrived. Now she was working in the kitchens and was,

by all accounts, both popular and a model employee.
Patrick had seen her and Helena taking nightly walks
down the drive, and he suspected Bronwyn was trying
to help the heavyset woman lose some weight. Obesity
had always troubled her because of the way her mother
had died.

"Well, we both know," Patrick said. "But I don't
know myself how a person goes about doping horses."

"Does it make them faster or slower?"

"I think both have been done."

"So my dad had someone give a horse something to
make it slow, and then the people who bet on the horse
lost their money."

"That's my understanding," Patrick said. "But I'm no
expert, as I told you." And Ari Theodoros's crimes were
so numerous that Patrick had been disinclined to look
at any of them closely. Because of his own vocation,
he'd been most interested in some insider trading from
which Ari had benefited. He glanced at Wesley. He
could see Bronwyn's bone structure and something of
her elfin facial expressions in the boy. "What are you
thinking, mate?"

"I wish I could give those people back their money.
The people my father cheated. Because they didn't get
their money back, did they?"

Patrick felt awed—awed by the complexity of this
child, by his obvious sense of honor, by his thoughtful-
ness toward the victims of his father's crimes. "They

didn't," he admitted, searching for something to say that might help Wesley. "But returning their money— I don't know how that would be possible, Wesley. It wasn't your crime, and you and your mother aren't being allowed to enjoy the rewards in any case. Your father's assets were seized. And some people might argue that the people who lost money were gamblers— and therefore prepared to lose."

"Would you say that?" Wesley asked.

"I would never say it was right or okay to cheat them," Patrick told him. "But it wasn't you who did it, Wesley, and it wasn't your mother."

"Why did he?"

"Your father? Why did he participate in illegal activities?" Seeing that this was what Wesley meant, Patrick considered at length. "I think that for those of us who don't do those kinds of things, who wouldn't consider it, why someone breaks the law is baffling."

"He hurt people."

Patrick sensed that they were venturing further into waters for which he had no charts. "By taking their money?" he asked.

"I heard my mum talking. People's lives were ruined. Some of his friends went to jail, too, and one of their wives had to go to a special hospital for people with mental problems. And little people, too."

"Little people?" Patrick listened carefully over the clopping of the horses' hooves, trying to understand.

"I heard someone talking, one of their friends. Or he used to be. He said to my mum, 'Neither of you care about the little people.' I guess he meant children."

"I think he meant people without money or power," Patrick corrected. "And in your father's business, there were people with less power than he had—and, yes, they may have suffered for his actions."

"I want to fix that. I want to fix it all for him, because he can't fix it now. When he went to jail, my mum said that maybe he would learn from the experience, but now he can't learn because someone murdered him. And I think he was murdered by someone he thought was a friend, and my mum thinks so, too."

As did virtually everyone. Not *by* a friend, but on the orders of someone whom Ari Theodoros had counted as a friend.

Wesley continued, almost as though speaking to himself, "I think I knew he was doing something dishonest. I mean, I didn't *know,* but I sort of did know, if you understand."

Patrick read between the lines. "There's nothing you could have done to change him, Wesley, neither you nor your mother."

Wesley gaped up at him, as though found out.

"He was an adult," Patrick told him, "and he made firm choices. I'm sure that nothing either of you said or did could have dissuaded him from going on with the life he had made for himself."

"My mum was mad when she found out. And she was sick, too. She tried not to let me know, but I knew."

So Bronwyn had suffered for her choice. Well, he could have guessed that.

"I'm sure you miss him," Patrick said, because it must be true. Whatever his own feelings about Ari—both as the man Bronwyn had chosen over him and as a criminal—Patrick knew that this young boy must still feel love for his father.

"Sometimes I didn't see him that much," Wesley said unexpectedly. "I liked it when he'd take me places with him. Sailing. Or to the racetrack. We went there once."

"Would you like to go to the racetrack again?" Patrick asked.

"My mum didn't like him taking me there."

Patrick wondered if Bronwyn would see things differently now that she worked for Fairchild Acres.

"She didn't like me exposed to the gambling," Wesley explained, using curiously adult phrasing.

"Well, if I took you to the track," Patrick said, "we would go down to see the horses. That's the reason to enjoy Thoroughbred racing. To watch the horses, because they're great athletes."

"I didn't like horses at first," Wesley admitted. "But now I like to watch the morning gallops before school, while my mum's working in the kitchens. I like that horse Indecent Proposal. I like to watch him run."

"So do I," Patrick admitted.

"And I like Meadow Boy. Can we canter now?"

Patrick, Patrick, Patrick, Bronwyn thought exhaustedly that night. She'd listened to Wesley chatter all the time he was getting into bed. *Patrick this* and *Patrick that*. And still she hadn't told Patrick what she was doing at Fairchild Acres. He hadn't asked again, and she was relieved to keep the matter to herself, relieved not to have to face his reaction to the news that Wesley was his son.

Not yet, anyhow.

The evening was warm, and she stepped out onto the porch, then wandered through the twilight toward a paddock where three horses stood. One was Meadow Boy, whom Wesley rode and to whom her son had introduced her. Now, the old horse came toward her, apparently recognizing her, and Bronwyn reached out to touch his nose. Where would any of them be without animals? All humans needed touch, and for some, touch was hard to come by. During her second walk with Bronwyn, Helena confided that she hadn't had a boyfriend for three years.

After Ari's deceit, rushing into another relationship wasn't the number one priority in Bronwyn's life. As she grew older, she found it was other relationships she valued most. Friendship, motherhood. Because happily ever after hadn't worked out that way, and now she was no longer certain it existed at all. Not in love and marriage. Perhaps simply in living and working and loving the people around her.

"You haven't ridden since you've been here, have you?"

She jumped—and knew who had spoken even as she spun to face him. She quickly turned back, focusing on the horses. The two others had followed Meadow Boy to the fence. "I'm a kitchen employee," she said. "I didn't come here expecting to ride."

"Didn't bring any boots?"

She had brought riding boots, simply because she was going to a place with horses. That didn't mean she expected to ride. "I did," she admitted and quickly changed the subject. "Thank you for taking Wesley riding." Now was the time. Tonight, out here, unheard by others, she could tell Patrick the truth. "He enjoys your friendship," she said.

"Would you like for me to arrange a horse for you to ride?"

She mustn't become sidetracked. She must say it now, say it while they were on friendly terms. "It doesn't matter," she said, formulating the words she wanted to use.

"It always worries me when people say something doesn't matter."

"What do you mean?" In spite of herself, she glanced up at his profile, her eyes lingering on his finely cut jaw, on the chin and lips and all the features she'd once loved and still found so terribly attractive.

"It's a bit like saying life doesn't matter," he replied. "Isn't it?"

"Life matters," she assured him.

"Is it so bad without Ari?" he asked kindly.

"No. No, not exactly." She had been asked about her feelings so seldom since Ari's death. People simply ascribed to her whatever they thought she ought to feel: anger at his betrayal, grief over his death. Her real feelings were so much more complicated—and always colored by worry. "I just never expected to find myself in this position."

"Having to feed yourself."

She wheeled, preparing to defend herself from another attack on her personal ethics.

Instead, he touched the side of her face, his own expression infinitely compassionate. "For you especially, the way you grew up, to be suddenly homeless with a ten-year-old boy must be terrifying."

There was no arguing with this. Bronwyn didn't know the name of the process which had shaped her in life or caused her to feel as she did now. She just knew that nights on the street, encounters with other homeless people who were too often drunk or mentally ill, had been frightening for the child she'd been. Yet she'd grown used to the fear. And the fact of adjusting to constant danger, constant fear, had changed her forever.

She would always react with horror to the thought of being on the streets again. Her first reaction was never: *I've done it before. I will survive.* It was, simply, *No! No! Don't let it happen!*

Well, she wasn't on the streets. She was at Fairchild Acres, and Patrick Stafford was cupping her jaw, his fingers threading her silky tresses. And then he kissed her.

Touch. Touch. Touch.

Yes, being near horses and dogs was well and good, but Bronwyn found herself hungry for *this* touch. She felt as though the kiss was giving and reaffirming life in the face of Ari's death.

She needed to feel this alive. She touched his chest, her fingers feeling the silk of his button-down shirt.

Patrick felt only half-conscious, only half-sane. This was Bronwyn, Bronwyn whom he had once loved so much, Bronwyn whom he still desired. And she, it seemed, desired him.

Yes, that's how it seems. He heard his own doubts, and he understood the depths of those doubts within himself. She couldn't still desire him. Not after all this time. And she'd married Ari. Which meant...

He drew back, confused by his own action and by Bronwyn's response to that action. He could hardly accuse her of seducing him. She hadn't sought him out, after all. Not tonight. On the contrary. He'd come looking for her and found her.

But now she was gazing up at him, her eyes startled, wary.

He remembered the impact of her beauty upon him. He said, "This was your goal, wasn't it?"

"What?" She blinked, appearing to come out of a trance.

"You wanted this to happen," he said. "Between us. Again."

"That would have been foolishly optimistic on my part," she said. And yet she withdrew from him slightly, perhaps taken aback by his accusation.

Or perhaps because his accusation had been correct.

"I don't know how you thought that it would be all right for you to work here and for you and Wesley to live here," he said. "I still don't understand your motivation, but I know what has to be done about it, Bronwyn. You need to get out of here. Both of you."

Bronwyn reeled, her mind sifting through his words, trying to make sense of them. "What do you mean?"

"I mean, I'm sacking you. You need to leave."

"But you didn't— You aren't even the one who hired me."

"My great-aunt has granted me the power to make personnel changes. Would you like to defend yourself to her?"

Bronwyn couldn't believe her ears. He was firing her? She hadn't even received her first paycheck, and

Wesley had barely started school. And she had planned to tell Patrick….

But it would be crazy to tell him the truth about Wesley. If he was capable of doing something this uncalled-for, making a pass at her and then firing her because the attraction was reciprocal… Had he just intended to trap her?

Obviously. She couldn't speak, didn't know what to do. Until now, it had never occurred to her to beg Patrick Stafford for anything. "I need this job," she said, and heard the desperation in her own voice.

"I've no doubt you can find something that pays better in Sydney or elsewhere. Something that takes advantage of your educational experience, such as it is."

"Why are you doing this?" she asked. "What have I done to you? What has Wesley done?"

"You've come to where I live, sought contact with me and tried to seduce me for your own ends, Bronwyn."

"I beg your pardon?" Thank God she'd never told him the truth about Wesley. If Patrick was capable of putting this slant on the events of the last week, then how could she trust him with influence on her son's life?

And if he wasn't to be trusted…

Yes, she may as well go.

So she turned away from him in the dark, appalled by what had happened. The hypocrite, she thought. Suddenly, she couldn't resist spinning back to him and saying it aloud. "You know, I've heard rumors that you and your sister only showed up here to get your hands on Louisa Fairchild's money."

Patrick stiffened. This was a rumor he hadn't heard, but who would have told him? Like most rumors, it had an element of truth. "I don't have to answer you," he began by saying, finding that internally he was shaking with rage. He kept his exterior steely calm. "But I'm going to. Maybe you can carry the truth back to the gossips in the kitchen."

"I never said—"

He cut her off. "Louisa is our great-aunt, Megan's and my only family besides each other. I love her. When I came here, it was because of the rift between her and my mother and grandmother. And yes, I came representing the interests of my ancestors. I felt that Louisa had stolen my grandmother's share of Fairchild Acres. That was how I saw it. Now, I'm simply grateful for the chance to know Louisa. In the past weeks, she's been accused of murder, had a heart attack and almost seen everything she owned destroyed by fire. She doesn't give up. I can't help but love and admire her. Believe it or not, having found Louisa and discovered who she really is—that's worth more to me than all the money on earth." Unable to stop, he said coldly, "Have you ever loved anyone like that, Bronwyn?"

She ignored the taunt—and his insistence that he'd come to love Louisa. "It's always been my understanding that people can leave their property to whomever they please. Why did you think it should just be divided between two sisters?"

"I've told you it's moot now. But if you want an answer, that's the way I would do it."

Very interesting, Bronwyn thought. "So when…if… you have a child, you'll leave all you have to him. Or her," she hastily added, but felt her irritation rising. How dare he fire her!

"That's correct," Patrick said. "And if I have more than one child, my estate will be divided equally between them. Favoritism creates bad feelings. If there's one thing every child needs, at every stage of life, it's the assurance of parental love."

"I'm glad you see your responsibility so clearly," Bronwyn said, and enunciated slowly and carefully, "because you, Patrick Stafford, are a father."

Stillness. Patrick heard a horse snort in the paddock.

It was as though he'd been kicked in the gut, had the wind knocked out of him. He couldn't speak.

It's a trick! This is the trick she planned.

And yet how could Bronwyn expect to trick him in this day and age, with paternity so easy to establish beyond a doubt?

She was smarter than that.

"Thank you," he said coolly, "for telling me."

"I didn't intend—"

"Because I will certainly want to claim my parental rights. All of them. And Wesley may have spent his life

until now with you, but I question the maternal capa-
bilities of a woman who can lie to a child about who
his father is, who can lie to her husband about the
identity of the biological father. I assume you did lie to
Ari?"

"I didn't know. At first I didn't know. He looked like
a baby. I just—"

"I find that hard to believe," Patrick said. "It's a fact
that human infants resemble their fathers. There is a biological imperative in this. It convinces the father that the
mother is not concealing the kind of thing you con-
cealed from Ari. Not to mention me. It assures the father
of a child that he's looking at his own offspring. Tell me,
Bronwyn, in a way I can believe, that you truly believed
Wesley was Ari Theodoros's son."

"I didn't say that. I said I didn't know." Bronwyn regretted her rash announcement. He was angry, which
she should have expected. She should never have told
him in the way she'd chosen. "Patrick, I intended to tell
you differently."

"When? After I'd promised to support *you,* as well
as him?"

"I think you should stop saying these things." She
spoke slowly and clearly. "Because you're saying the
kinds of things I will find it difficult to forget. No doubt
you've always believed I married Ari for money. And
now you're deluding yourself that I would tie myself to
you for the same reason. If you believe either of those

things, then you don't know me, Patrick Stafford. And you never have."

A chill went through him, and it had little to do with the knowledge that he was Wesley's father or with the thought that Bronwyn had kept the fact from him until now. It was a dim sense that perhaps he had said unforgivable—and unforgettable—things. "I'm upset," he said quickly. "I've probably said things I don't mean."

She sensed a slight capitulation on his part. "Patrick, I came here to tell you. This is why I came. I was going to tell you tonight. Then—"

Then I kissed her, Patrick thought.

Then he'd fired her.

But he didn't want Bronwyn Davies around anymore. Wesley, yes. Wesley was a wonderful boy, his boy, and Patrick wanted him near. His affection for the child had grown so much in the short time Patrick had known him; and now he felt pride that this extraordinary boy was his son, as well as an immediate sense that he would do anything, anything, to protect and nurture Wesley.

He believed Bronwyn's explanation of why she'd come to Fairchild Acres. It made more sense than his suspicions, which he now saw had been little more than wishful thinking. *Patrick, you conceited—* She'd just done a decent thing. Belatedly, yes.

He knew he should tell her she wasn't fired, that she could keep her job. He'd been an ass. Louisa would go through the roof if she heard how he'd behaved tonight. And, as usual, Louisa would be entirely right.

But he couldn't bring himself to take back the rash edict.

Instead, he said, "Look. Let's leave this for now. My lawyers will look into this. If Wesley is my son, I mean to provide for him and be a father to him. If that's what you came here hoping, that's what you're going to get."

It was what Bronwyn had come to Fairchild Acres hoping. But she didn't like the sound of "lawyers." When custody suits went to court, money won. Her impulse was to take Wesley and flee—tonight, if possible. Hadn't Patrick just fired her? Now she was unemployed and homeless. That would look really good to a magistrate.

Keeping her fears quiet, she said, "I came here hoping Wesley could know his father." A father he could admire. But was Patrick Stafford really such a great role model? Bronwyn wondered now.

You can pick 'em, Bronwyn, she told herself bitterly.

Patrick said no more, and so she turned away and headed for the employee bungalow.

Once again, she and Wesley had no home.

And Wesley's father, the man she'd come to Fairchild Acres hoping he would grow to know and love, was responsible.

Chapter Six

Patrick lay awake, alternately considering his recent interactions with Wesley, feeling satisfaction with the person his son was—and no little sudden love for him, as well. Bronwyn had done a fine job. It had to be her influence. Patrick would have expected a child growing up surrounded by Ari Theodoros's wealth to have a certain arrogance and sense of entitlement. Even in his own parents' much less affluent household, Patrick and Megan both had grown used to receiving the material things they wanted, had even taken those things for granted. But Wesley wasn't spoiled, was in no way a whiner, had excellent manners and took a simple joy in soccer, in riding Meadow Boy.

Yes, Patrick believed that telling Wesley that he was his son was the reason Bronwyn had come to Fairchild Acres. That didn't mean, however, that she didn't have another agenda behind the revelation—maybe something which she hadn't acknowledged even to herself. Fact: She was hard up for money. No doubt she'd at least hoped that he would help support Wesley, which Patrick was more than willing to do.

He told himself that he was tossing and turning on his bed's memory-foam mattress because he was excited to learn that he had a son. After all, he'd always wanted children. It was only finding a suitable woman to marry and be their mother that had been a problem.

And why is that, Patrick?

He wasn't afraid of the question. He asked himself if he had believed in some subconscious way that no other woman could measure up to Bronwyn.

He tossed that answer around for a bit.

Well, the other women he'd met *had* failed to measure up to her in one particular way. Other women— his sister and Louisa excluded—seemed bound to tell him what they thought he wanted to hear, rather than simply what they thought.

Certainly, he'd never marry a woman who refused to see herself as his equal. No such woman could really capture his mind and heart.

What about fear of rejection, Patrick? Could that be part of the reason you're not married?

It had been a sobering, miserable experience to be turned down by the woman he'd loved, who'd also announced her engagement to a different man by saying that her fiancé's values more exactly matched her own.

Yes, that had been bad.

He made himself think of Wesley again and was terribly excited. He wanted to call Megan, to tell her the news that he was a father, the father of a marvelous boy, a boy who could face down a brown snake without going to pieces, a boy who wanted to make reparation for Ari Theodoros's crimes, a truly extraordinary young person. Yes, Wesley was exceptional.

And Louisa would be delighted. She already had a bit of a relationship with the boy. Wesley had told her the story about the snake and Beckham's defense of him. Louisa had told Wesley that they must do something to reward the dog, and she'd obtained a fabulous bone from the kitchen for Wesley to give Beckham. Yes, Louisa's heart was already won by Wesley.

Patrick nearly groaned at the thought of how Louisa would react to the news that he'd fired Bronwyn. *I shouldn't have done it.* Not because of Louisa's likely reaction, but simply because it had been wrong. He was going to have to take it back, to make sure that she stayed.

Because if she stayed, Wesley would stay. In fact, Wesley should have his own room in the big house. Patrick began considering what sorts of things Wesley would most want in his room. Did he have favorite possessions stored in Sydney? Most probably.

He finally rose from his bed and walked into the hall. Perhaps the room Wesley had occupied the first night he'd spent at Fairchild Acres would be the right room. Or the bigger one his mother had used. Patrick grabbed a pair of sweatpants, pulled them on and slipped out of his room, prepared to think about the possibility.

Bronwyn stared moodily at the shadow of the lamp on the wall of the living room. She hadn't been able to sleep, and had instead packed her belongings then grabbed a book that Marie had lent her. It was an American paperback called *Red Sky at Morning,* which unfortunately was very much a father-son story, and she stared at the same page for twenty minutes.

She heard a doorknob turn, and a moment later a sleepy Marie Lafayette wandered into the hallway and then the living room, blinking at Bronwyn.

"What are you doing up?" Marie asked. "I saw the light."

"I could ask you the same," Bronwyn replied.

Marie sighed. "I get—preoccupied. Things on my mind."

Bronwyn considered this. It had occurred to her more than once that Marie had some history she wasn't keen to reveal. But Bronwyn's attempts to get her housemate to talk always failed to produce any earth-shattering revelations. Marie's mother was dead, had died suddenly, and usually when Bronwyn asked what was troubling her, Marie simply responded that she was thinking about her mother.

Having lost her own mother in the way she had, Bronwyn could understand this preoccupation.

And, to be fair, she'd never confided in Marie.

But now, what was to be lost?

Wesley didn't know Patrick was his father. And Bronwyn wasn't sure how to tell him. Yet there was something about Marie that assured Bronwyn this woman would not let the truth slip. Marie was, quite simply, trustworthy. Bronwyn liked her, respected her maturity and valued her friendship.

"Oh, hell," Bronwyn finally breathed. "I have to tell someone." And so she told Marie, in whispers as the beautiful, elfin blonde sat beside her on the couch at the edge of the room. Marie looked alternately horrified, outraged, concerned and consoling.

"The thing is," Bronwyn said, "he's powerful. He has money and he's related to Louisa Fairchild. I'm no one. And I've already seen that he's paranoid and vindictive."

"Probably more of the former than the latter," Marie replied. "Don't you think it's likely wishful thinking on his part that you came here hoping to ensnare him? And I'm sure he knows it. He doesn't seem that dishonest to me—dishonest to himself, I mean. He acts frightened."

"Of what?" Bronwyn demanded in disgust. Without even considering her own question, she whispered, "I'm the one who's frightened. I heard him, Marie, when he started talking about getting his custodial rights. And he has fired me. So what's to lose by my taking Wesley and getting out of here as fast as I can?"

"Potentially, a lot," Marie said. "First of all, I think you would have a hell of a time hiding from him. These people are powerful. Also, his firing you was completely unjustified. I've watched Louisa Fairchild a good deal since I've been here. You could say that I've studied her. She won't stand for what Patrick has done. She has a reputation for being hard-nosed, but she's fair. Her integrity is important to her."

Bronwyn considered this. "But he's her blood."

"I don't think that's going to matter. I happen to know she basically cut her sister out of an inheritance, threw her out of the house, that kind of thing."

Bronwyn remembered hearing that. It was hardly a state secret, especially around Fairchild Acres. There was a definite feeling that Louisa Fairchild harbored no shame about her decision. But it didn't strike Bronwyn as a fair one, so why should the woman be fair to her, a stranger?

"I don't think you should run," Marie said. "It's not fair to Wesley. And it has to count for more than a little that Wesley has spent his entire life until now with you and barely knows Patrick."

"And he doesn't even know Patrick is his father. God, I hope Patrick thinks about that before he does anything crazy."

"*You'd* better tell Wesley," Marie said. "The sooner the better."

"I can't think about that right now. Wesley loves Ari's memory. Oh, God, it's all so tangled."

"Sir Walter Scott said something about that, didn't he?" Marie mused, but as though she were speaking more to herself than to Bronwyn. And thinking private thoughts again.

"Something about what a tangled web we weave when we set out to deceive. But that was never my plan. It just sort of happened."

Marie spared her a sympathetic look. "What I think you should do, Bronwyn, is try to get your job back."

"How?"

Marie frowned. "I think you should tell Mrs. Lipton that Patrick fired you. She'll be annoyed at having to hire someone new."

"But what shall I tell her about the reason why?"

Marie pursed her lips. "The truth would be interesting."

"That Patrick Stafford first made a pass at me and then fired me?" Bronwyn felt a slightly evil smile spreading across her face.

"I want a word."

Louisa Fairchild's eyes spit venom in Patrick's direction. Clearly, his great-aunt was incensed about something. Patrick himself was focused on the computer at his desk. It had occurred to him that Wesley had probably never doubted Ari Theodoros was his father. Which made telling Louisa the facts a more complicated proposition. Patrick had started out the day with work, as usual, online. Then he'd begun researching soccer camps, thinking Wesley might enjoy a week at such a place. "What's happened?" he asked.

"A word," Louisa repeated, her stance making it clear that she wasn't going to share his attention with his computer monitor.

Patrick stood and said, "I suppose it's breakfast time."

"I haven't the stomach for it at the moment," his great-aunt said, enunciating each word slowly and carefully.

Patrick realized uneasily that he was the focus of her anger. What had he done? Granted, what he'd done the previous night with Bronwyn—but that had been a private scene. Had Louisa discovered…

"Since when," Louisa demanded, "have you felt it was your right to make sexual advances to the help and then fire them to cover up your behavior? That is sexual harassment, Patrick, and I'm *astonished* at you."

To tell the truth, he was astonished at himself, but Louisa didn't give him the chance to say so.

"I don't care if she's your old girlfriend. I wouldn't care if she was your ex-wife. That is no way to treat an employee."

"You're—" *Right. You're right.* But before he could get the second word out, she pounded on.

"She is a single mother, and you fired her without cause—except your own lack of self-control in her presence. Is that what I'm to understand?"

"I—" He fell silent.

"Yes?" Louisa said. Without waiting for an answer, she told him, "Well, you can march right out to the cottage and rehire her, Patrick Stafford. And may you never act like such an ass again, or you'll find yourself excused from this property." Eyes stormy, she added, "A widow trying to raise a ten-year-old boy alone, and you were going to throw her out of her home and cost her all her income."

Patrick knew that the news that he was Wesley's father would only incite Louisa to greater ire. The recipient of his bad behavior was the mother of his child. Quickly, he said, "I apologize."

"You owe apologies to *her,*" Louisa said, without denying that she'd been owed any.

"I'll rectify the situation immediately," he said. "Would you find it adequate if I promoted her?"

"I think you know," she said with a very nasty look at him, "exactly the behavior I expect of members of this family. *That* behavior will be adequate."

Feeling about four feet tall and ten years old himself, Patrick said, "I'll just…go out to the bungalow. Right now."

"You just do that little thing."

* * *

Bronwyn's posture as she rocked in the paint-peeled chair on the bungalow's porch, the picture of anxiety, served only to triple Patrick's shame. He had stopped in the kitchen to speak with the chef, to admit that he'd done something rash with regard to Bronwyn Davies, and to ask if perhaps she was ready for a promotion from dishwasher. So now he was prepared to face her.

"I'm sorry," he said when he reached her. He did not come up on the porch. Keeping his distance was doubly important now—no more scenes like last night. "I behaved appallingly. I'm ashamed of myself—both for taking advantage of you and for firing you without justification. I've had a royal telling-off from Louisa that was fully deserved. And I've spoken to your supervisor in the kitchen. You've been reinstated and promoted to prep cook and dietician, if you're willing to accept your new role. There has also been a suggestion that a new position be created as staff fitness trainer. This is something I will bring to Louisa's attention."

Bronwyn stared at him. Her fearful posture didn't seem to lessen. She said only, "Thank you." Then, quickly, "Wesley's at school. Patrick, he doesn't know. And this whole time has been traumatic for him already."

"I gathered as much."

"Could I ask you please to keep things…quiet? I'm

not telling you to tell no one—just to be discreet, so that Wesley doesn't learn the truth casually?"

"Just when do you plan to tell him?"

"I'm not sure. I'm just not sure. But—not today. Please. Too much…at once."

"I *am* going to be part of his life, Bronwyn."

"I hope so," she said.

Patrick gazed at her, unable to keep from reflecting how beautiful she was—and how much he had wanted her when they'd kissed. He could no longer pretend to himself that Bronwyn hoped to seduce him. Yet he longed to kiss her again, to feel her kiss him with the passion she'd once shown. He wanted to touch that honey-colored skin, to cup her cheek, her finely formed jaw, in his hand. He wanted to taste her tongue, to be intimate with her as they had been once.

Part of him believed that such passion must be based on true love—perfect love. Another part of him knew that history—that life itself—was rife with situations of unrequited love or simply a love that was stronger on one side than on the other. In fact, that was often the most likely scenario.

Regardless of the responsiveness he'd convinced himself she'd shown the night before, it was more likely that she felt nothing at all for him. While he…

Just garden-variety attraction, Patrick. You're not in love with her.

Nonetheless, he'd expected a warmer response to

the reinstatement of her job—no, to her promotion—than she'd given.

Well, now she'd let the cat out of the bag, and he was going to do everything he could to enjoy a full part in Wesley's life, to be the father the boy deserved. He would get joint custody of the child—any court would allow him that.

Irritated that Bronwyn wanted to stall telling Wesley the truth, Patrick asked again, "When do you plan to tell him? It would be traumatic, don't you think, if he learned the truth by accident?"

Her green eyes seemed to shoot sparks. "And how exactly could that happen, Patrick? As far as I know, only you and I know the truth." She deliberately overlooked the fact that she'd confided in Marie. "I'm certainly not going to let that information out accidentally, and I trust you'll take the same care."

"Bronwyn, you must know that I'm going to have to talk to an attorney?"

"Why?" The cry sounded hoarse, high and weak. A cry of fear.

"To arrange custody," Patrick told her.

"I'm not going to deny you time with him," Bronwyn said, pale now and sounding desperate.

"We'll still need to put something in writing. This is the way sensible people do things, Bronwyn."

"Sensible people who don't mind submitting innocent children to the pain of court battles."

He cocked an eyebrow. "But you just said you're not going to deny me time with him. Why should there be any battle at all?"

Bronwyn bit her lip and didn't answer. Instead she rose from the rocker. "I'd better get ready to report to the kitchens." She took a breath that was visible rather than audible. "Thank you for your—" She seemed unable to finish the sentence—or to meet his eyes.

"For being reasonable?"

She finally gave a small nod, which seemed to say that what he'd said was not precisely what she wanted to express, but the best that could be managed under the circumstances.

"I regretted firing you as soon as I did it, Bronwyn. I was a jerk." Some impulse of honesty or of generosity made him add, "And Louisa was outraged. She's a very decent woman."

"Better than," Bronwyn agreed, and turned away to go inside the bungalow. Patrick watched her long hair swing behind her and told himself that what he should really focus on was finding a good attorney.

The head chef, François, was now Bronwyn's immediate supervisor. He was fiftyish, bald, short and a bit round, but extremely charming. He flirted mercilessly with Bronwyn and Marie, yet seemed to treat them both as young cousins, as well. He was protective and generous with advice on everything from grades of butter to fashion.

From the first, Bronwyn enjoyed her new position. Though François and she occasionally were at loggerheads on what was suitable to feed an elderly woman with a heart condition, he did seem interested in her nutritional advice.

"But tell me this," he would argue, "why is it that the French women have less cellulite than you Australians with your diet?"

Bronwyn couldn't help saying, "I'd be happy to pose my butt beside any Frenchwoman's, François."

Laughing, the chef said, "*Oui,* but you are the exception, you and Mademoiselle Lafayette."

Bronwyn saw Helena's face fall into an unhappy expression where she stood dicing celery.

Bronwyn edged over to her housemate and whispered, "And you're next. You look great, Helena."

"I wish the weight would come off faster."

Helena gazed unhappily at the vegetables she was slicing. "More protein, less fat," she muttered as though it were a mantra.

"Ah, Helena." Unexpectedly, François appeared beside them. "But you have the body and face a Dutch master would paint. What do these skinny things know of true beauty. It is you—*you* who makes an old man's heart pound."

Bronwyn bit down a smile. Helena was thirty-two and the chef quite a bit older, but sometimes she thought she saw a special spark between the two. And Helena had supplied the interesting information that she and François had once attended a wine tasting together and that she had visited his charming loft, above a carriage house at one of Hunter Valley's nearby wineries.

Bronwyn tried not to worry about Patrick's determination to involve at least one lawyer in custody issues with Wesley. She also tried to forget the event that had led to his firing her the other night.

He'd kissed her.

The kiss had taken her into stormy waters. Her own response terrified her. She'd *liked* it. And then he'd behaved so cruelly. Then so kindly the next day.

If she was honest with herself, she found him even more attractive than she had when they were younger. Now he was steady, mature, strong in himself. But Bronwyn didn't want to rush into another relationship with anyone. At Fairchild Acres, she was discovering an independence she hadn't known since before she'd married Ari.

And she liked it.

Marie joined her at the counter, where Bronwyn was noting the day's menu in a laptop provided for kitchen record keeping—another move, Bronwyn was sure, for which she could thank Patrick. "How are you doing?" Marie said softly.

Bronwyn cast her a look. Guiltily, she remembered what she'd said to Patrick two days earlier—that he and she were the only ones who knew the truth about

Wesley. She'd confided in Marie. Not that she doubted the other woman's discretion, not for a minute. Still, she'd lied to Patrick, not wanting to reveal her conversation with Marie in the small hours of the night.

Bronwyn murmured, "Things seem okay so far."

There was enough noise in the kitchen to muffle their conversation.

"Is there any chance the two of you might ever, you know, get back together?" Marie asked.

"I don't want to get together with anyone." She made herself warn, "Marie, you know how important it is that Wesley—"

Marie seemed to understand what Bronwyn left unsaid. "I wouldn't make a slip like that, Bronwyn. I do know."

And Bronwyn felt a reinforcement of the trust she'd placed in Marie Lafayette.

The bantering behind them in the kitchen seemed to lessen somewhat, and Bronwyn glanced around to see Louisa Fairchild standing in the kitchen doorway.

Fear coursed through her, and yet she didn't know why she should be afraid. Was there any chance Patrick had told Louisa the whole truth?

But Louisa's eyes were right on Bronwyn's as she said, "I need to borrow your prep cook, François."

Casting a nervous glance at Marie, Bronwyn started for the kitchen doorway.

Louisa said crisply, "Please come with me, Ms. Davies."

* * *

Fearfully, Bronwyn followed the Fairchild matriarch out of the kitchen and toward the stairs that Bronwyn knew led to the wine cellar.

What is she going to do to me? she thought, fighting an inappropriate desire to laugh.

"Miss Fairchild, I want to thank you for—"

Louisa spun so fast that her agility stunned Bronwyn. "For what?" snapped Louisa Fairchild.

"For my promotion," Bronwyn said softly. *For standing up for me.* But she couldn't say that much, afraid of family loyalties, afraid of speaking aloud things of which Louisa might not want to be reminded.

"That was Patrick's doing." The old woman turned on the light at the head of the stairs leading down to the cellar. "He's also brought to my attention that your university training might help qualify you as a bit of a personal trainer for my staff. I suppose for me, as well, if I wanted such a thing." Louisa seemed to pause as though considering whether perhaps she did want or need such a thing. "He pointed out that some of the staff really don't seem to take the care of themselves the way that they should, and also that Fairchild Acres is a modern business and ought to offer its employees the best perks. I agree with that assessment. So—" She continued down the steps, making her way slowly, grasping the handrail.

Bronwyn didn't dare offer to assist, but remained ready to reach out and grab the woman if she should fall.

Rather than continuing down the stone passage which Bronwyn knew led to the wine cellar, having been sent down there in the past to retrieve wine for dinner, Louisa turned down another passage and groped for a light. She switched it on.

The glow fell on a hardwood floor and some dusty weight machines.

"Fool things have hardly been used," Louisa said. "Don't even know if they work. My former head groom wanted to set this up for the jockeys, but no one ever really used it. So, I want your guidance. I hear you've been teaching yoga or something of the kind in the living room of the bungalow. What would you need to set this up as a better facility?"

Bronwyn gazed about her. Fluorescent light fell on a spacious room which nonetheless had a cold, unused feeling. There were, however, a couple of high windows which must be at ground level. She wasn't sure what to say.

Practicality took over. "How much do you want to spend?"

"I think it should be a state-of-the-art facility. The grooms and jockeys will use it if they have professional guidance, and I'd like you to offer classes for the kitchen and housekeeping staff, as well."

"You'd like me—" Bronwyn's voice trailed off.

Louisa was giving her a look that seemed to shout, *Isn't that what I just said?* "Right then," she said quickly. "Mirrors, for a start."

"Would you be up to making me a list and perhaps looking into purchasing equipment we might need, as well?" Louisa said. "I'm sure Patrick would be happy to assist you in terms of answering any questions you have."

"Certainly," said Bronwyn uneasily.

"Rest assured, he will be making no more unwelcome advances," Louisa told her crisply, but in a tone that discouraged Bronwyn from replying to that particular remark.

"I can do it," Bronwyn said.

"I'm afraid François may have to make do without you in the kitchens," Louisa added, almost as if to herself. "I think your new role will be too time-consuming, running our physical fitness facility and teaching classes. In fact, I will make your excuses for you now and leave you here to start thinking." Louisa's cane thudded as she turned to leave the basement room.

But Bronwyn wasn't comfortable letting the old woman climb those stairs alone. She had a feeling that letting Louisa know, however, would earn her a tongue-lashing. She thought fast.

"I don't want to say it…."

Louisa spun again, facing her sharply. "Yes?"

"Well, there may be a problem if a lot of employees have to use these stairs…." Bronwyn started toward them.

Louisa did not follow at once, and Bronwyn was afraid her employer scented subterfuge. So she made a deal of squinting up at the dimly lit stone steps.

At last, she heard Louisa's cane and light step behind her.

"For instance—" Bronwyn walked up the first three steps "—places like this here." She pointed out a dip in the natural stone.

Louisa made a thoughtful sound and started to climb the steps after her.

Bronwyn pointed out small imperfections in the steps, examined the lighting over the stairs. She was sure she'd fooled Louisa—until they both reached the top.

There she found Louisa giving her a penetrating glance. "You're a clever girl, aren't you?" her employer said, and turned away without a word on what improvements the stairs did or did not need. But she added, without looking back, "I'll send Patrick down, shall I?"

It sounded to Bronwyn a bit like revenge.

Chapter Seven

Patrick found Bronwyn in the basement, writing on a steno pad he recognized as one of those used throughout Fairchild Acres by staff. She'd twisted her long hair up in a loose knot, and she seemed to be checking the weight-training equipment. She glanced up as he entered the room. Her cheeks flushed.

Patrick saw.

Did it mean anything, that sudden infusion of color?

But her tone, when she spoke, was businesslike. "Good. I guess I do need some guidance in terms of what Louisa is likely to think reasonable in the way of—"

"'Whatever she wants,' were her words."

Bronwyn frowned, eyebrows drawing together as she peered up at his face. "Why?"

"What do you mean, why?"

"Why does she want to spend so much on something that she seems to have tried before and which didn't work out?"

"Well, I guess because she feels she didn't put the energy into it that she should have last time. She really wants someone on the premises who can help the jockeys and grooms and the rest of the staff keep in shape to prevent workplace injuries, that kind of thing."

Bronwyn wasn't sure she believed this explanation but chose not to voice her doubts. Instead she said, "Well, I guess the next thing to do is make a list of the staff who will be needing to use the facility and an assessment of their needs."

"What do you need, Bronwyn?"

The question startled her. She shot a look at him. "What do you mean?"

"Just what I said. I think Louisa wants to meet your needs, as well."

"I always make sure my needs get met," Bronwyn said stiffly. Then, afraid of how Patrick might react to these words, she said, "A home for me and Wesley. That's what I need, and it's what I have." *For now, anyway.* It was still hard for her to trust Louisa Fairchild's largesse.

"Did Ari meet your needs?"

She would have thought he was taunting her, except that his voice was serious. Also, she sensed he wasn't talking about money—or about physical needs. She asked, "Emotionally?"

"Yes."

She swallowed, not wanting to answer. "I was in love with him. There were times that were all joy, when we really seemed to be one. But you and I were such friends, Patrick," she finally said.

"And you and Ari weren't?"

"That's not what I meant. But we weren't contemporaries. That's what I chose, intentionally chose, but sometimes…" Sometimes Bronwyn had longed to be with someone her own age, to share in the same generational experience. Someone who'd seen the same movies and television shows, who'd grown up playing with similar toys. Which wasn't to say her and Patrick's childhoods had ever been socially similar.

"You chose him because he was older?" Patrick said, sounding as though he doubted this.

"Yes," she answered. *Because he was mature.* Which Patrick hadn't been—not then. Half-desperately, she said, "Patrick, you and I are Wesley's parents. I know you feel bitterness toward me, but please don't let that—" She didn't know how to continue.

Patrick gazed at her until she lifted her eyes to him. "Don't let it what?" he asked.

"When you can't forgive someone it poisons you." She

gave a rueful laugh. "I should know. I'm spending a lot of time these days trying not to poison myself that way."

"Because of Ari?"

Bronwyn didn't answer directly, but said, "And he had as much or more to forgive, though he never knew it."

Wesley, Patrick thought. "He never guessed?"

"If he did, he never said." Then she remembered Ari, remembered how he'd really been. "And he wouldn't have let that go," she admitted at last with a sigh.

"But you want Wesley to keep thinking that Ari is his father."

"Not forever!" Bronwyn objected. All her fears rushed back to her—above all, the fear that Patrick might try to take Wesley from her.

Patrick tried to guess the source of her anxiety. Only the previous afternoon, he and Wesley had gone riding yet again. Patrick had taken even more satisfaction in the experience than before, knowing that this fine boy was really his own son. But he had kept his word to Bronwyn and let no hint of the truth reach Wesley.

Bronwyn said, almost to herself, "I'm afraid. Afraid of how it will affect him. Afraid he'll be angry with me for lying to him all this time, even though it was for his own protection."

"Protection?" said Patrick incredulously.

Bronwyn seemed belatedly to register her own words. She appeared dumbstruck.

"Why should it have been for his—"

"Ari wouldn't—" She clamped shut her mouth.

"So he wasn't so nice."

"He always was," she insisted. "I just knew that—" But what had she known? She'd known nothing. She'd never suspected Ari was a criminal. And yet she must have sensed some ruthlessness within him, something that had made her fear grave repercussions if he'd learned that Wesley wasn't his natural son. Well, any man would have been angry about that.

She closed her eyes. "I didn't know of anything specific he'd done. I didn't know he was a criminal. But part of me must have suspected what I didn't know. Does that make sense?"

"Actually, it does," Patrick answered.

He sounded understanding. She gazed up at him, wishing that what she heard could be true—that he actually *did* understand.

"I think when we love someone, we resist seeing specifics," he said. "Maybe we resist seeing the truth. That can happen unconsciously. I had a partner once...."

"What?"

"A business partner. I haven't thought about him for a while. He did some things which, while not illegal, were unethical. I managed for some months to not know. I say managed, but I'd swear it was all unconscious. And yet, when the truth suddenly stared me in the face, I realized that in fact I'd always known."

He *did* understand. She'd been able to confide her confused feelings about Ari to Patrick and he had so completely understood. Her heart filled with warmth. The moment reminded her of something past, something gone like childhood but sweet to recall. And yet it had just happened. Was there some ghost of friendship left between her and Patrick?

"Thank you," she whispered, as much to herself as to him.

"For what?"

For being my friend. In the past and in these last few minutes. But Bronwyn couldn't utter the words. She was too afraid to hear him refute them. "I'm really excited about this job," she said instead.

But Patrick, watching her look down at the notes she'd been making, suspected that she wasn't thanking him for anything to do with the job.

Ordinarily, Dylan Hastings would not have been the first person Patrick would choose to confide in. But he couldn't very well ask Louisa if she knew of any good divorce attorneys. Louisa would ferret out the truth about Wesley in a heartbeat.

Besides, Dylan had been through a divorce of his own.

So Patrick was pleased when Dylan, Megan and Heidi stopped by the following day before Heidi headed back to school. While Megan and Heidi went out to the stables so that Megan could say goodbye to her horse, Patrick and Dylan sat on the porch, each with a beer, and Patrick tried to work out how to get the information he wanted from Dylan without breaking his promise to Bronwyn.

He settled on the old "a friend of mine has a problem" approach.

He wasn't sure Dylan bought the story of Patrick's old friend from university who'd learned unexpectedly that he was a father and was looking for a good attorney to help him secure his parental rights. At one point, Dylan said, "And how old is this child?"

"Ten," Patrick admitted with some reluctance. He thought he saw something like amusement cross Dylan's features, but whatever Megan's fiancé suspected, he didn't put it into words.

Finally, Dylan said, "What does your friend want out of the situation?"

"Parental rights," Patrick answered as though this were obvious.

"What rights, though? Visitation?"

"Half time. I know he doesn't want a court battle or anything like that."

Dylan's look was strangely grim. "Well, it's all fine to talk about fifty-fifty time, and some people are in favor of parents just working things out for themselves. But as someone in law enforcement, I recommend getting everything in writing."

"That's what I thought," Patrick agreed. He would

have to tell an attorney everything, but the attorney would be bound by client confidentiality.

"Sure, I have a guy I'd recommend," Dylan said at last. "But I have to say, your friend's lucky that the kid's mum wants to be with her child."

"Of course she does," Patrick said, then remembered that this wasn't the case with Dylan's daughter, Heidi, whose mother didn't seem to know or care what happened to her daughter. He opened his mouth to apologize, but Dylan seemed to intuit Patrick's realization of his mistake.

"No worries," Dylan muttered. "She's got Megan."

Patrick heard the love bordering on reverence with which Dylan spoke of Patrick's sister. It made him like the other man, went some distance toward forgiving him for ever having suspected Louisa of murdering Sam Whittleson.

The attorney Dylan recommended was named Everett Wyatt, and Patrick liked him at once. The lawyer had a mild manner and revealed at the first meeting that if Patrick was looking for a ruthless attorney who didn't care who he damaged in order to secure his client's rights, then Patrick was talking to the wrong man.

"My first case," Everett revealed, "was a wrongful death suit, and it taught me a lot about the law, people and time. You spend eight years in court, there goes your son's childhood. In my first suit, these people wanted to sue for what had happened to their child, but by the time it got to the courts four years had passed. In the normal course of events, they would have begun to heal—not to get over it, because you don't, but to heal. Well, going to court stirred everything up again, really prevented their moving forward."

Patrick realized he'd had the good fortune to discover an attorney who was not only fair, but wise.

When he had told Everett everything—even down to his making a pass at Bronwyn and then firing her—Everett twisted his mouth a bit. "Is the mother going to fight you on this?"

"I believe she thinks she's prepared to be fair, but when push comes to shove, she'll probably hang on tight. She's resisting telling the boy the truth."

"And you're going along with that."

"You don't think it's the right thing to do?"

"I think it's absolutely the right thing to do. Let her know that the boy is going to have to know the truth, but don't blurt it out to him yourself. Sounds like he doesn't need that kind of trauma. He thinks his father was a criminal, and the man's just been murdered—frankly, you might want to look into getting the kid some counseling when he is told.

"And you did the right thing to give Mum back her job and see her promoted, because what you did doesn't look too good. I'd be very careful not to trouble her with any more unwelcome advances."

Patrick knew he was hearing good advice and felt doubly foolish for having made that pass at Bronwyn.

Everett pulled a legal pad toward him and began scrawling. "All right, let's get everything down, so we can serve Mum with some notice of your intentions."

Patrick spoke slowly, hesitantly. "You don't think maybe I should just...try to talk her into things."

"Under the circumstances," Everett answered, not bothering to look up, "absolutely not."

"Which circumstances?"

"The circumstances that your recent behavior could easily be construed as sexual harassment."

"I *am* going to have to work with her."

"Then keep it professional."

Patrick arrived back at Fairchild Acres to find Louisa in high gear about a barbecue she wished to host the afternoon before an upcoming race at Warrego Downs. Patrick could scarcely follow her conversation, her waspish remarks about both candidates for president of the International Thoroughbred Racing Federation, her requests for his opinion on where marquees should be erected to minimize guests being troubled by the burned-out smell from the recent fires.

He wanted to say that those smells would be in his own nose the rest of his life. He had a sudden fearful vision of Wesley riding alone and confronted by wildfire. Snakes, spiders, sharks, skin cancer, every peril of the world suddenly loomed large as he gazed upon his environment as a parent.

My son... That Wesley was his son with Bronwyn made the child all the more precious to Patrick. Wesley was what endured of his long-ago love affair with Bronwyn. Bronwyn, who was still more surpassingly beautiful than any woman Patrick had ever met or known.

His mind on Bronwyn, he hurried down to the basement. He knew she had already started teaching three classes in the new recreational facility. One was an aerobic conditioning class, another was yoga and the third was Pilates. She had already asked Patrick if he thought Louisa would allow her some time away from Fairchild Acres to obtain more training. She wanted to be certified as an instructor of Iyengar yoga and a Pilates teacher.

Patrick was beginning to get the feeling there was nothing Louisa wouldn't do for Bronwyn. He'd actually heard Louisa say the fatal words to Bronwyn: "It's a pity you don't have a more extensive riding background." From Louisa, that was as good as saying, *If you'd been my child...*

It was a compliment, a sign of Louisa's caring and concern. The same kind of concern Louisa had shown toward Wesley.

Patrick found Bronwyn working out in the basement, lifting weights, using the bench and weight machines that had arrived that morning. In the corner of the room were six spinning bicycles for indoor cycling classes.

But Bronwyn wasn't alone. Two of the other workers were with her—her housemates Marie and Helena. Patrick had learned Helena's name when he had referred to her as "the heavy one" to Bronwyn. Bronwyn had snapped, "Her name is Helena, and she's lost ten pounds in the last two weeks, *and* she's extremely strong."

That had put him in his place—and increased his affection for Bronwyn. That made him uneasy. He found her attractive, and he admired her compassionate and professional desire to help Helena and the other employees. Plus, she was already working with Louisa on some easy exercises that would increase the older woman's mobility. He'd looked for signs that Bronwyn was sucking up to her boss and had found none.

Marie eyed Patrick as he came in. A strange one, that woman. Quite good-looking, but he always had the feeling that she had amassed a wall of secrets behind that elfin facade.

Not his problem, in any case. She said to Helena, "Ready, Helena?" and he saw that the two women had just finished their workout.

Helena was on the scale. "One second."

"Not right after exercise," Bronwyn told her. "And stop being obsessed with that damned thing."

"Yes, Mum," Helena laughed. The two women waved to Bronwyn and departed.

Bronwyn eyed Patrick warily.

Well, he had his orders from his attorney. Keep it businesslike.

"Just wanted to check on the things you ordered, see if they came in and if everything is satisfactory."

"Quite," Bronwyn told him. She picked up two towels from the floor and took them to the hamper, then tilted one of the spinning bicycles on its casters to move it out from the wall.

"Where is our son?" Patrick asked.

"A riding lesson. From your sister, actually."

"Ah." He wondered how the meeting between Bronwyn and Megan had gone. They'd always liked each other. When Bronwyn had turned down his proposal and he'd told Megan why, his sister hadn't condemned her. It was only Bronwyn's acceptance of Ari that had raised Megan's eyebrows.

Bronwyn looked him up and down. She nodded to the bikes. "Care to join me? You'll want to change."

She was reaching out to him, offering friendliness. Could accepting that offer be considered something other than professional? Of course not.

"I'll change and be right back," he said, hurrying out of the room.

What had made her invite him to do this with her? Bronwyn asked herself as she moved a second bicycle out into the room. She knew the answer. It was those moments of friendship the other day, when he'd shown he really did understand what she'd known and not known about Ari.

How had she come to value friendship so much? And it wasn't just friendship; Patrick was an old friend, the person who knew her better than anyone else at Fairchild Acres, except, possibly, Wesley.

And he's attractive, Bronwyn.

That was exactly what she couldn't afford to notice or care about.

In minutes, Patrick returned downstairs wearing a pair of cycling shorts and a T-shirt. "I prefer to ride outside ordinarily," he said. "There's a nice road past the Kay vineyard. Do you have a bicycle?"

"No. I mean, I did in Sydney. But we had a bit of a sale before I left. I needed to put some money together—" She stopped abruptly.

Patrick wondered if she was hypersensitive to his opinion of her financial situation. Maybe she was afraid he would lash out, accuse her again of trying to worm money from him.

Truth be told, he no longer suspected her of such behavior. Since Louisa had confronted him and given him that piece of her mind about his treatment of Bronwyn, he'd been forced to look harder at himself and to realize how childish his behavior had been. And now he knew the real reason Bronwyn had come to Fairchild Acres. He believed what she'd said, that she wanted him to know Wesley and for Wesley to know him. So he said lightly, "Louisa has a couple of bicycles in one of the outbuildings. Sometimes the employees use them."

Bronwyn lifted her eyebrows and gave an agreeable nod. "Then, maybe I'll get to do some outdoor cycling, too."

As he adjusted the seat of the bicycle beside hers, Patrick said, evenly and cautiously, "Please try not to take offense if I ask again when you plan to tell Wesley the truth."

Bronwyn glanced at him, her expression wary. She said, "I don't know. I don't know how to do it, and, to be honest, I'm terrified he'll hate me when he learns the truth."

"Hate you why?"

"Think about it. For lying to Ari, for lying to Wesley. He'll probably just be terribly confused, and this has already been such a traumatic time for him."

"Because of Ari's murder?"

"Of course. On top of learning more than I wanted him to know about his fath— about Ari's criminal background."

"I spoke to my attorney today."

Bronwyn shot a look at him. She began pedaling, and soon he was pedaling the other stationary bike beside her.

"He suggested that counseling might be helpful, so that Wesley can come to terms with these changes."

"Wesley doesn't need counseling," she snapped.

Patrick lifted his eyebrows. "You just said—"

"But he doesn't need to talk to some stranger."

"You think you're all he needs for his mental health, then?"

Bronwyn heard the challenge. "I listen to him. He has no mental health problems. He has just been through a bad time."

"What are you afraid of, Bronwyn?"

She was afraid of someone trying to take Wesley from her. It was that simple. She could imagine some psychologist speaking to the courts, making it seem that she had been a bad mother to Wesley. She was afraid of the power Patrick wielded because of his wealth and her poverty.

She was terrified of the situation she'd married to avoid, the situation in which that mistake had now landed her. She said, "What are you asking for?"

"Fifty-fifty," he said. "Half time with him, of course. Anything different would be wrong."

"He's a ten-year-old boy, and you think being away from me half the time will be good for him?"

Again he saw the anger and fear flashing at him from her green eyes. "It seems fair," he said. "And I think he needs to know me, as well, as you yourself have pointed out."

She fell silent, pedaling furiously. Standing up on the pedals, she said coldly, "Let me show you the three positions you use in spinning class. Since you're doing this, you may as well get the best workout I can give you."

* * *

Patrick sensed he'd made a mistake with Bronwyn by telling her about his meeting with the attorney. He might be feeling positively toward her, but her wariness had increased; she'd become more aloof.

As the weekend barbecue approached, he still had occasion to see her as she prepared the fitness facility. He came down to help supervise workmen hanging the new floor-to-ceiling mirrors, and he even came to a couple of Bronwyn's yoga classes, where she'd treated him with remote courtesy.

By Friday afternoon, as the entire staff of Fairchild Acres welcomed the first guests to the barbecue, guests who included both candidates for the ITRF presidency, he wished he could take back any mention of the attorney. Of course, Bronwyn would have received the papers the day before. The attorney had sent Patrick his copies, and he had spent time reviewing them just that morning. Was Bronwyn right that it was unreasonable to expect Wesley to live with him half time?

"Patrick, I want a word."

He turned from a table he had been helping to move and found Louisa scowling at him. What had he done this time?

He followed her to the house where she marched into the downstairs study.

There, she closed the door behind him, walked to her

desk and lifted up a sheaf of papers. "Please tell me the meaning of this."

He saw the letterhead on the paper and flushed. "I don't think that correspondence is addressed to you." Was she even reading his mail?

"I stumbled upon it when searching your desk for papers you promised to retrieve for me about Andrew Preston's campaign."

"Maybe," he said coolly, "the best idea would be for you to pretend that you didn't see it, then."

"Bronwyn Davies's child is your son?" Louisa demanded as though she had not heard him.

Patrick was surprised at the shot of alarm he felt. It had nothing to do with Louisa's wrath—or his own. He spoke quietly. "Wesley himself doesn't know, and I have promised his mother to keep the fact confidential for the time being. So it might be a good idea if you kept this information inside this room."

"And you want fifty percent custody of the boy or time with him or whatever word you use for it?" Louisa demanded.

"It seems only reason—"

"What it is," she told him in a rough whisper, "is appalling. You're trying to take a child from his mother while under my roof."

"Not trying to take—"

"Fifty percent? When he has spent one hundred percent of his life at her side? And she is his *mother.*"

Louisa imbued the word with almost spiritual overtones. "You would take him from his mother?"

"What are—"

Unwilling to let him get in the questions he wanted to ask, she said, "Have another think, Patrick Stafford. That will not happen under my roof. You have outlived your stay if you think I'll countenance someone removing a child from his mother's home. Fifty percent. Do you think he's a time-share condo?"

"I think he's my son."

"Then you might learn a quick lesson in decency toward his mother. Hear this, Patrick. You have money. That poor girl has none. No doubt you think you're going to get your way with expensive attorneys, bullying her into relinquishing her parental rights, all because she chose another man over you."

"This has nothing to do with—"

"Well, it won't work. I can hire attorneys, too, and I will. If you try to take that boy from his mother, you won't be fighting Bronwyn Davies's purse—you'll be fighting mine. And *me*. If you want to know your child, I suggest you figure out how to stay in his mother's good graces. And try showing her a little respect."

Interfering— Patrick cut off the thought. "Fine. What I want, however, is your word that you'll mention this information to no one else."

"And I won't have them out in the employee cottage. They're family."

"Yes, but Wesley doesn't know that. You need to slow down here, Louisa. I want Wesley up here, too, but Bronwyn doesn't want to spring the truth on him."

Louisa said, "Very well. Of course, I'll say nothing. Except, perhaps, to her." Thoughtful, she glanced toward the windows looking out on the stables. "There's Jacko Bullock. If only I could trust that man."

Chapter Eight

"Boss wants you," Helena said, looking in the door of the gym.

Bronwyn had lost some of her fear of Louisa Fairchild, but not all of it. Louisa treated her so well, more than fairly, and yet strangely that only served to increase her trepidation in the woman's presence. She supposed it was because the fair treatment increased her own sense of responsibility toward Louisa. Bronwyn expected more of herself, knowing that she had been treated generously.

She had been reviewing a DVD on repetitive motion injuries, with an aim to helping one of the grooms, who was also under a doctor's care. Bronwyn had borrowed one of the Fairchild Acres utes earlier that day to accom-

pany the groom to an appointment with his physio-
therapist. She knew that she was expected at the barbecue upstairs. Fortunately, she'd already changed into
some classic ivory slacks and a silk blouse, with a
choker of pearls, her wedding gift from Ari, around her
throat. So much of her jewelry from him she'd pawned,
but the pearls held happy memories. She felt no guilt in
having those memories, and was more disturbed by the
part of herself that hated him for his crimes.

She shut down the large-screen monitor and DVD
player, turned off the lights and left the room that had
become the center of her world. She was so happy at Fairchild Acres now. As soon as he arrived home from school,
Wesley hurried through the kitchen and downstairs to
join her. Then, Bronwyn would accompany him upstairs
to make his snack, look at his schoolwork and hear about
his day. If she had no classes, she played soccer with him.

Or else, he rushed off to the stables to go for a ride.

With Patrick.

Louisa Fairchild was waiting in the hall at the top of
the stairs.

When Bronwyn joined her, the old woman turned on
her heel. "Come with me." Walking swiftly with her
cane, Louisa led the way through the house, through the
elegant living room with its tasteful antiques—nothing
cluttered or fussy—past photos of horses, horses,
horses, and into the room which Bronwyn had learned
was Louisa's office.

As Bronwyn stepped through the door, Louisa said, "Please close that."

Uneasy, Bronwyn did as her employer asked.

"I have learned through no fault of Patrick's—he has honored your trust—that Wesley is Patrick's son."

Bronwyn's heart fell. She'd felt powerless enough confronted by Patrick's wealth. If Louisa Fairchild set out to help him take Wesley from her, how could she possibly fight them?

"I've also learned that he hopes to secure fifty percent time with Wesley."

Bronwyn said nothing.

Louisa glared at her. "I've told him that I won't countenance such a thing. No one on this property is going to gain my support in taking a child from his mother. Even," she added when Bronwyn would have spoken, "for half the year. Patrick knows that if he chooses to fight you on this, he will also be fighting me."

"You?" Bronwyn felt faint. She was also moved—touched—but thought she must be misunderstanding Louisa. "I don't want to come between—"

"You're not coming between Patrick and me," Louisa said. "Though I've known them only a short time, I have a fierce loyalty to Patrick and Megan. But you, too, are family, as is Wesley. You both have a home at Fairchild Acres. Forever."

Part of Bronwyn—a sentimental part of her that she'd thought long since dead—grew warm with feeling. Her eyes started to flood, and she blinked quickly, remembering the suspicious nature that had become part of her as a teenager and had been strengthened by Ari's perfidy. Was Louisa Fairchild trying to exert power over her? Was she being used?

Bronwyn whispered, "Why are you doing this?"

Louisa gazed at her hard, seeming to struggle with a private battle. The old woman said, "Children belong with their mothers. Patrick obviously didn't know that I have strong feelings on this subject. Now, however, he does."

"Thank you for your kindness and generosity," Bronwyn said, still unable to completely dismiss her doubts. There was no such thing as a free lunch.

"I want you and Wesley here in this house."

"I don't want to be treated differently from—"

"But you are different, my dear. You're family."

"But Wesley doesn't—"

"Yes, Patrick told me. Wesley doesn't know the facts."

"Miss Fairchild—" Bronwyn began.

"Louisa."

"Louisa, I—I'm grateful, but I'm used to—I need to work. I can't accept something for nothing."

"Who said anything about your not working?"

Bronwyn felt herself flush. "I meant, you've already been more than good to me. If I can just continue as I have been—"

"You don't wish to live in this house? Even knowing it might be better for Wesley?"

Bronwyn thought this through. Better for Wesley? Well, Patrick lived in this house, that was true.

"I don't want the other women," she said, "my housemates—"

"You don't want to set yourself above them," Louisa said thoughtfully. Something complex seemed to be unfolding behind her eyes, part memory, part something else. Finally, she said, "I suppose if I'd ever been given the choice whether or not to be set apart as a Fairchild... Yes, I might have preferred to fit in with everyone else, too."

"I appreciate your trusting me," Bronwyn said. "Not thinking that I'm like Ari—"

Louisa gave a snort. She gave Bronwyn a wave of her hand. "Well, we'd best be part of this barbecue."

Bronwyn froze. "You're not hoping—" She stopped, knowing that what she'd almost said might be considered impertinent.

"Not hoping what?"

"Patrick and I—it was a long time ago."

"You think I'd sell you off to him? No, Bronwyn, that's between the two of you. And, considering the things he's done, if you think him an ass, that's quite all right with me."

Patrick saw Bronwyn emerge from Louisa's office ahead of his great-aunt. He gave her a tentative smile. Bronwyn's eyes met his for a moment, and she flushed.

Why? he wondered. Louisa must have told her that she had nothing to fear from him.

His own feelings were a tumult, and he wondered if, now that Louisa had announced her intention to fight his suit for Wesley, he could safely ignore his attorney's advice and be less than professional with Bronwyn. He nearly shuddered as he imagined Louisa's reaction if she could read his thoughts. All right, he could be professional but also…friendly.

He said, "Everything all right?"

Bronwyn cast another look at him. "Yes."

She looked distrustful. Of him? Of Louisa? But how could she trust, after what had happened with Ari. She'd trusted that her husband was who and what he'd pretended to be, and look what had happened.

She paused beside him and looked up. He'd met few women with green eyes and none with such a clear green as Bronwyn's. He thought of Wesley, who held both Patrick's and Bronwyn's genetic heritage. A product of their love, for they had been in love back then.

"Want to join me outside, get something to eat? And where is Wesley?"

"He and Beckham were going for a walk last I knew. Wesley's trying to teach him to retrieve."

Patrick nodded. Louisa had stepped out through the French doors, and now Patrick and Bronwyn were alone. "When are we going to tell him, Bronwyn?"

"I don't know," she whispered. "I think I should tell him alone. I don't know how he'll react, and that will give him the most privacy with his feelings."

"Perhaps this weekend?"

Bronwyn considered.

"Will you come to the races with me tomorrow?" Patrick asked.

Bronwyn's face once again betrayed uneasiness and suspicion. She seemed terribly fragile to Patrick.

He said softly, coaxingly, "I'm asking you on a date."

A date, Bronwyn thought. A date with her former lover, with the father of her child, with a man who had asked her to marry him yet had seemed unready for marriage.

But Patrick wasn't that person anymore. In the past few days, she'd watched not only his interaction with Wesley, but with Louisa and all the employees. During one indoor cycling class, he'd even lightly flirted with Helena, marveling at her strength and endurance, and Bronwyn had seen Helena flush with pleasure at his encouraging compliments.

Yes, this new Patrick, this different Patrick, was someone she wanted to know better. But only if she could do so without surrendering her independence. "I suppose," she said slowly, "there won't be any classes."

"It's settled then. An Indecent Proposal is going to run. He's my favorite."

"And *the* favorite, from what I understand."

Bronwyn found herself walking out into the warm afternoon sunlight with Patrick. She felt comforted and safe, as though she'd just put on her favorite nightgown or oldest, most comfortable pair of shoes. But outside she spotted photographers, members of the press come to report on the social occasion, and she immediately saw one camera point at her.

She swung away in half-forgotten practice, remembering cameras outside the flat in Sydney, outside their various other houses. She was attractive and had been married to Ari Theodoros, and she had no doubt that members of the press recognized her.

A protective arm went around her shoulder, and she hissed, "Don't. It will make it worse." More cameras flashing.

"Mrs. Theodoros. Do you feel welcome here among the Thoroughbred set?" one journalist asked.

"This is a party," Patrick said. "Ms. Davies is a friend of the family and an employee here. If you harass her— or anyone else—you'll be asked to leave."

Bronwyn spotted Jackson Bullock, and a host of bad memories came back. She'd never liked the man. Ari had been one of his supporters, and Bronwyn had been surprised that the doping scam hadn't netted Bullock along with so many others. She had no wish to draw the man's attention.

"This is awful," she told Patrick. "Where's Wesley?" She turned and started away from the patio and the food and down toward the employee bungalows. Patrick fell into step beside her.

"When are you going to move up to the main house?" he asked.

"I don't think that's appropriate," she replied. "Wesley and I are fine where we are."

"I wanted to ask you. Next week I need to go to Sydney, and I was hoping you and Wesley would join me. There are spare rooms in my penthouse. I'm trying to get tickets to a Socceroos game."

This is going too fast. "That's very nice," Bronwyn said, "but I'm needed here. There are classes to teach, and I'm helping one of the grooms with his physical therapy."

"Patrick!" Wesley barreled up to the two of them, Beckham at his heels. "Watch what Beckham can do." He threw a ball. "Go get it, boy!"

Beckham chased the ball, caught it, brought it back and dropped it at Wesley's feet. "Want to play soccer, Patrick?" Wesley asked.

"Actually, I want to make sure your mother gets something to eat."

"Food," Wesley said excitedly, as though he'd just realized the barbecue was in progress. "And tomorrow I'm going to the races. Louisa said I could, if it's okay with you, Mum."

"It's okay."

"We're all going," Patrick told the boy.

"Hooray! Come on, Beckham. Let's go to the barbecue."

"Don't let him steal food or jump on people," Bronwyn warned.

"I won't, I won't."

"He seems happy," Patrick observed as the boy raced toward the food tables.

"He does. The happiest he's been since Ari was arrested."

Patrick revealed to Bronwyn some of the feelings Wesley had confided on their rides together.

"He wants to pay for Ari's crimes," Bronwyn murmured. "It's going to confuse him no end to learn that you're his father."

"You might be surprised. He's obviously very resilient."

"I have to tell him sometime. I don't know why it feels best to wait."

"Perhaps because you don't trust me?"

Bronwyn glanced up at him. In truth, the person she didn't trust was herself. She loved her new life at Fairchild Acres. She wasn't ready to enter into another relationship which might jeopardize her independence in any way. But what Patrick seemed to be offering looked damned attractive. She liked him, and it would be so tempting to yield to the kind of security a partner offered.

Well, she was getting ahead of herself. He'd only

asked her to the races and to come to Sydney. It all might be because of Wesley.

She found herself saying, "I trust you, Patrick."

Bronwyn dressed carefully for the races the next day. Marie had the day off and would be accompanying them.

"I feel silly going on your date with you," Marie admitted as she and Bronwyn checked their reflections in the mirrors in the bungalow.

"Well, I feel better with you going," Bronwyn said. "Besides, they're all pretty nice. Patrick's sister will be there."

"Why did you marry Ari? I mean, you'd been seeing Patrick."

"Ari was very romantic. When he showed up, he seemed like exactly what I'd always wanted. Patrick wasn't the way he is now. He was a student and had very vague plans for the future. I couldn't count on him. I loved him, but I felt bad for loving him, because I knew he wasn't serious about making a living. Maybe not even about making a commitment. He'd really never had to fend for himself in the world."

"Well, he's definitely past that," Marie remarked.

"Yes, but back then, he was a history student. It seemed so impractical. Everything about him was like that."

"Ah." Marie looked thoughtful, but said no more.

Bronwyn, trying to fill in the silence, wondered if

she really had made a mistake all those years ago. If she'd stuck with Patrick, would he have become the man he was now?

Frankly, she doubted it.

But she felt flashes of anger at Ari, who had married her and yet at his death had left her and Wesley in such a mess.

"He's doing it. He's doing it." Louisa, eyes fixed to the track with the aid of binoculars, was watching An Indecent Proposal's progress. "Hold off, Teddy, hold off," she whispered to the jockey. "He knows his horse," she said to Bronwyn, who stood beside her, without lessening her focus on the track. "Yes, yes, yes."

Seconds later, a celebration erupted in the box.

While champagne was being uncorked, Louisa suddenly drew Bronwyn aside. "Patrick's going to Sydney next week," she said, "and I think it's a good time for you to get some of that training you wanted. I noticed a course for that type of yoga you want to teach, and Patrick says you're welcome to stay at the penthouse with him."

Bronwyn couldn't stop herself from asking, "Do you have an ulterior motive in this, Louisa?"

"Nothing secret," Louisa replied. She flashed a look that included Wesley and seemed to say that Wesley's parents belonged together.

Patrick handed Bronwyn a glass of champagne and

met her eyes. "So. Will you and Wesley come to Sydney with me?"

Bronwyn nodded, wondering why the prospect didn't make her happier. But she knew the reason. She didn't like other people making decisions for her, and she detested the thought of being financially dependent again. She'd depended on Ari, and she was happier now, with only herself to rely on. Marrying Ari, she'd traded independence for what she'd believed was security. Now that she had her independence back, she was loath to relinquish any part of it again.

On the drive to Sydney in Patrick's Range Rover, they listened to *The Hobbit* on tape. By the time they arrived at Patrick's penthouse apartment, Wesley was trying to make riddles of his own to match the game Bilbo and Gollum had played. Beckham sat beside the boy on his seat, and Bronwyn heard Wesley ask the dog, "Would you have guessed any of those, Beckham?"

The book on tape had been Patrick's idea, and Bronwyn was impressed. *He's already a good father.*

Patrick's apartment was spacious, furnished in a simple, clean style Bronwyn most liked. He had fantastic views, including one of the Sydney racetrack. Beckham leaped up onto the couch first thing.

"Off!" Bronwyn said. Then, to Patrick, "Has Louisa been here?"

Wesley hauled the dog off the couch.

"No." Patrick looked toward the racetrack. "But I'd like her to stay here the next time one of her horses runs on that track. I'm very fond of her, Bronwyn. You weren't far off in your suppositions of what first brought me to Fairchild Acres. But soon it wasn't about the money at all. I began to care for Louisa, and Megan desperately wanted to be close to her. Our parents' deaths hit her worse than they did me. She wants family. She lives for family. Which is why Dylan and Heidi are so good for her."

Bronwyn thought about this.

"Come on, mate," Patrick told Wesley. "Let's have a look at your room."

Wesley followed Patrick in to a spacious bedroom and glanced around. He looked somewhat glum.

"What is it?" Patrick asked, noticing his expression.

Bronwyn, who'd followed them to the doorway, could guess the answer. It was so much like Wesley's old room, reminding him of his former life in Sydney. "Mum, could we call Colin?" he asked.

"An old friend from Sydney?" Patrick asked.

"Wesley, we're guests—" she began, eyeing Beckham as he sniffed a nearby table and wandered toward the kitchen.

"Yes," Patrick answered Wesley. "I want you to feel like this room is yours. No one else uses it, and you and your mother will be coming to Sydney more frequently now. As a matter of fact, we should look around for some things of your own to go in it."

Bronwyn bit her tongue. Patrick was keeping his word, not telling Wesley the truth about who his father was. So why did she feel uneasy?

He's taking over.

Yet she wasn't sure she really believed that. What was Patrick doing but trying to make Wesley happy? And hadn't Wesley known enough unhappiness for any ten-year-old boy?

Patrick tossed Wesley his own mobile phone. "Why don't you give your friend Colin a call? See when you can get together."

Wesley had not forgotten Colin's number. He dialed.

Bronwyn said quickly, "I'll speak to his mother, Wesley." She was uneasy. Colin's parents hadn't liked their son spending time with Wesley after Ari's arrest. Bronwyn knew that they believed she'd been unaware of Ari's criminal activities. Nonetheless, there had been a definite chill. Perhaps they'd believed her appallingly naive—or simply stupid.

Patrick seemed to read her expression. "Tensions with old friends?"

She gave a barely perceptible nod. But a few minutes later she was on the phone with Colin's mother, making arrangements to pick up Colin after school that day. Hanging up, she said, "And speaking of school, you have some assignments to take care of, young man." Wesley's teacher had been flexible about his planned absence and had assigned several projects, one of which included a visit to the museum in Sydney, another to the zoo.

Colin accompanied them to the zoo.

At first, Wesley had felt strange with his old friend, afraid Colin would want to talk about Ari. But then they'd practiced football together. Colin had brought his ball, and he and Wesley played with it in the grounds of the zoo. "Let's go see the snakes," Colin said.

Beckham had stayed behind in the penthouse, being unwelcome at the zoo, but Wesley had told Colin about the dog. Now he said, "There was a brown snake in my bedroom in Hunter Valley."

"No way."

"Yeah, and Beckham was barking and growling at it. It was scary. Hey, I wonder if there's a mongoose at the zoo here."

"What's a mongoose?"

Wesley began to relax as he answered his friend. But when they were in the reptile house, Colin said, "My dad says your dad's a snake."

My dad's dead, Wesley thought. Why was Colin being so mean? He spun on his friend. "It's not true!"

"What's not true? You mean your dad's not a mobster? He didn't cheat people?"

Wesley remained silent.

Suddenly, Colin looked sorry. He said, "This one seems okay, though."

Wesley knew he was talking about Patrick, who had followed them into the room with Wesley's mother. Wesley saw his mother shudder as she observed an anaconda behind the glass.

"There's something wrong with a reptile getting that big," she said.

"Mum, tell Colin about the brown snake," Wesley said. "Patrick, do you think there's a mongoose here?"

"Let's find out," Patrick said.

Colin was right about one thing, Wesley thought. Patrick was okay.

There was no mongoose, but Wesley and Colin were both captivated by the zoo's binturong cub, Indah. The Asian bearcat was, Bronwyn had to admit, adorable. Her personal favorites were the red panda cubs, though. Patrick preferred the penguins and the tapir.

"He's weird-looking," Wesley commented about the latter.

"Maybe that's why I like him," Patrick told him.

They ate dinner at the zoo then dropped Colin back at his house. The following day, Bronwyn would start her yoga training program. When they returned to the penthouse, Wesley put Beckham's leash on him and took him downstairs for a walk, then set to work writing about the animals he'd seen at the zoo.

When it was Wesley's bedtime, Bronwyn read to him from a new book which Patrick had bought for him at the zoo, while Beckham lay on the floor beside the bed.

"Mum," Wesley said when she had finished.

Bronwyn looked at him.

"Colin's dad called my dad a snake."

Bronwyn tried to remember if she had ever called Ari a snake to her son. Considering the rage she'd felt during their desperate trip to the Hunter Valley, it was possible. Surely now was the moment to tell Wesley that Patrick was his father. Yet maybe it wasn't. He seemed in such pain already, confused and upset.

"I'm sorry," she said. "It must have hurt to hear that."

"But my dad was a good man, too, wasn't he? You always told me he was a good man."

And what can I say now? "Wesley, people are so complicated. I'm not sure it's up to us to say someone is good or bad. We can look at things they do and say, 'This is a good thing,' or 'That was bad.' But people? We can't know what goes on inside anyone. And sometimes people do bad things for reasons the rest of us can't understand."

"I love you, Mum."

"And I love you, Wesley."

When she emerged from Wesley's bedroom, Patrick had put a CD on the stereo. Allison Kraus and Union Station. A game box sat on the coffee table. "Challenge you to Scrabble?" he asked.

It was something they'd done in college. Actually, they'd been rather bloodthirsty about it.

"You're on," Bronwyn said with sudden enthusiasm, glad that Wesley's proximity made it impossible for them to discuss the need to tell him who his father really was.

"Tomorrow," Patrick said, "I have a couple of appointments. Since you'll be at your yoga seminars, I thought I'd take Wesley with me. There will be a place where he can be safe and supervised while I'm in meetings. Then, he and I can go find some fun—or maybe go to the museum, since we've promised his teacher."

"Yes, that's fine." Bronwyn had gotten first draw, first play. Her letters were a dream. *QUAFF*, with *Q* on the double letter and all on the double word.

"Revolting," Patrick said, noting her score. "As usual, you intend to win by a combination of unbelievable luck and unbelievable luck."

She stuck out her tongue at him.

He took more time with his choice and came out with a formidable forty-two points. "By the way, we'll want to look for an apartment for you while you're here. I do own two others, but they're both rented at the moment."

"Why an apartment?" she asked.

"Does that mean you're willing to live with me?" He smiled.

"No, it means I have a place to live, and so does Wesley. Fairchild Acres."

"Yes, that's my home base, too, now. But I'm going to need to be in Sydney some, and you should be here, too. I'm willing to help, but I'm not going to support you to the extent Ari Theodoros did."

Bronwyn's sudden rage was monumental. She sat back from the game board—perhaps to remove herself from the temptation of spilling the letter squares into his lap. "I think we've covered this ground, Patrick. You are not going to be supporting me. And Wesley will be remaining with me at Fairchild Acres. As your great-aunt and I have agreed," she continued acidly.

"It's worked out well for you," Patrick remarked.

Bronwyn tried to let that slide, suspecting what was behind his words. "Yes, it has. Let's drop this. We need to keep the peace over the coming week, so if you're entertaining bizarre suspicions about me or my motives, please keep them to yourself."

"Just as long as you remember that I won't up the ante." He changed his voice to a whisper, but looked directly at her as he uttered each of the next words. "Even if you continue to put off telling Wesley the truth."

Bronwyn had no idea how to disabuse Patrick of this strange belief that she wanted him to support her. "What makes you think that's what I want?" she asked, genuinely puzzled.

"Many things about people change—but not natures. You revealed your nature when you turned your back on your lover of two years and chose a playboy old enough to be your father."

Bronwyn was stung. "Let's just review this history you think you know so well. You asked me to marry you. I asked what you planned to do with your life. You said—" and she counted on her fingers "—one, you weren't sure. Two, you thought you might like to write, though once again, you had no idea what, whether it would be fiction, nonfiction or *poetry*." She stressed the last. "Three, when I said I was unwilling to support an artist, you told me that once you were successful you would then support me. I told you that was unrealistic, and I told you I had no fantasies about someone else supporting me. I wanted to make my own way—"

"Which you did, accepting the first multimillionaire who asked."

Bronwyn sighed. "What are you afraid of seeing Patrick?"

He pressed on as though he hadn't heard her. "Did you know you were pregnant?"

"I did not, and keep your voice down," she added. "Look, Patrick. I was in love with Ari. And, yes, the fact that I've never known my father probably had something to do with it. His money did not."

Patrick had gone white. But he didn't reply angrily, didn't seem to feel anger, not now. He seemed washed in some recollection.

Bronwyn focused on her Scrabble letters, trying to quiet her own anger.

Patrick studied her, but didn't see her. He saw the past, saw himself, a carefree university student, caught in the romance of other ages, thrilled by learning. That world seemed rich and many-layered to him. His parents had been stockbrokers till their deaths, and he'd thought their world paralyzingly dull.

But it wasn't. Once he had entered this world, he'd found it exciting and satisfying. Once he'd begun, he'd realized that he found tremendous fulfillment working with money. It was a game to him, one he enjoyed, and he was damned good at it. He was not a gambler. He simply knew what worked and what didn't.

He blushed as he recalled the things he'd said to Bronwyn. He'd become Megan's guardian long before he'd imagined really having children of his own. And he'd been annoyed whenever his sister had shown interest in men he considered impractical.

Bronwyn had never had a father to look after her interests that way, but she'd known how to look after her own. And instead of applauding her good sense, he'd spent the last decade thinking of her as a gold digger.

Because that had hurt less than thinking that she might love another man more than she'd loved him.

He didn't bother to say he was sorry.

Sorry didn't cover it. He was changed, changed by this conversation. No wonder she seemed to be putting off telling Wesley who his father was. She probably thought he was simply insanely jealous. Or something worse.

No wonder other women hadn't interested him over the past years. What other woman would have dared to speak to him so plainly? Only his sister, Megan, and even Megan was sometimes restrained by his being the older sibling.

No, only Bronwyn—and Louisa—had proven so willing to call a spade a spade.

He returned his thoughts to the game and finally settled by saying, "I hear you."

He thought she glanced up at him, but he couldn't meet her eyes.

He didn't want to, because now when he saw those eyes, only one thing filled his mind. He was falling in love with Bronwyn Davies, falling in love again.

Chapter Nine

The week passed quickly for Bronwyn, slowly for Patrick. Every night, he fought imagined visions of her in his bed. At the barbecue, Bronwyn had said she trusted him. But he doubted she trusted him enough to become his lover again.

So he enjoyed her and Wesley's company at a Socceroos game, at horse races and at an amusement park. Bronwyn actually sat between his legs on a roller coaster while Wesley's friend Colin sat with him.

When they returned to Fairchild Acres the following weekend, they found Megan, Dylan and Heidi visiting. Heidi had just finished a ride and showed an interest in Beckham. Soon, the children were playing with the dog, Heidi showing Wesley how to train Beckham to *stay* on command. Patrick invited Bronwyn to join him and Megan and Dylan on the patio for a drink, but Bronwyn begged off.

She wanted to get down to the physical fitness facility, see any changes which had been made in her absence. Also, she needed to distance herself from Patrick. After spending the week with him, she found the image of his face always before her, as though imprinted on her heart. He'd been kind, funny, fun to be with. And after their argument during the Scrabble game, he'd seemed reflective and had made no more accusations against her.

In fact, he'd been so kind and so much fun that she'd almost forgotten that stupid argument.

Her housemates were glad to have her back, and Marie wasted no time in saying, "So?" as though expecting romantic revelations.

"So, nothing. We bickered a little, but mostly got on fine."

"Got on?" Marie encouraged.

Bronwyn was reluctant to reveal her new feelings to anyone. She wasn't going to rush into a relationship with Patrick, and that was that. So she told Marie, instead, about their argument over the Scrabble board.

Marie frowned. "In that case, I hope you have at least some good news."

"Like what?"

"That you trounced him, of course."

Bronwyn laughed. "As a matter of fact, I didn't. I'd like to say that I was so annoyed it ruined my game, but the fact is, he has always been an excellent Scrabble player."

"Well, there's something else you should know," Marie said unhappily. At Bronwyn's questioning look, her housemate produced a tabloid showing highlights of the Fairchild Acres barbecue the previous weekend. There were several photos of Bronwyn, identifying her as "widow of late crime boss Ari Theodoros, implicated in racetrack fraud."

"Lovely," sighed Bronwyn, and was disgusted to find that the paper was local. "Poor Wesley."

"Oh, gosh, that's right," Marie said, looking horror-struck.

"I'm glad you showed me. Believe me, even in Sydney, his friends' parents had some trouble with their children playing with the son of Ari Theodoros. I imagine it will be even worse for him here."

"That's so unfair!" exclaimed Marie.

"Since when was life fair?"

Its unfairness made itself felt over the next few days as Bronwyn found employees who had initially seemed to like her now giving her a cold shoulder. Her exercise classes were less well attended, and no one but Helena and Marie ever stayed afterward to talk anymore.

"It will blow over," Marie said. "They know Louisa's not naive. I think it's just that what Ari did is so opposed to everything they stand for."

"And everything I stand for," Bronwyn remarked unhappily.

A face looked in the door.

Patrick.

Bronwyn took an exhausted breath, bid her two housemates farewell as they left the room, then turned her back on the door.

"What's wrong?" he asked.

She shrugged. "I don't think the employees of Fairchild Acres are keen to take fitness lessons from the widow of Ari Theodoros."

He was silent, and she did glance at him then, to see how he was taking the news. He looked stunned.

"Well, it's only natural," she said. "He was involved in doping racehorses. Anyone with integrity is going to find that despicable."

"That doesn't mean they need to find you despicable." He sounded indignant, and his indignation cheered her.

Then, she remembered that what she was experiencing must be nothing compared with Wesley's experience.

"What?" he said.

"What do you mean?"

"You just gave what I'd call a rueful smile."

"Ah." She didn't bother answering. At last she said,

"I'm concerned about how this publicity about my being Ari's widow will affect Wesley's experience at school."

"I shouldn't worry about it," Patrick said. "He's a good athlete and a handsome boy. He's made some friends already."

Bronwyn knew this. "I should have made sure he asked some of his friends over before this."

"You're a good mother," Patrick said.

"Thank you." There was no one from whom she would rather hear that assessment.

"Shall I speak to Louisa?" he asked. "Have her speak to the rest of the staff?"

"No," Bronwyn gasped, horrified at the thought. "No, people will just have to realize that I'm not Ari. Time will help them get over it."

"And trust you," Patrick finished for her.

"Yes."

"Bronwyn," he said, "I think there's really no reason to wait to tell Wesley the truth. The truth might help him at this juncture."

Bronwyn considered that for a moment. "I suppose I've been holding off because part of me believed you really think I'm mercenary," she admitted. "I've been afraid of you turning Wesley against me, negatively influencing how he perceives me."

Patrick looked stunned. "I wouldn't do that, Bronwyn. And you should consider that I've said some of the things I have to you because I was hurt that you chose Ari. In some ways," he added, "it was much more comfortable to tell myself that you married him for his money. But what you said in Sydney reminded me of the truth. You were right. I was unready for marriage then. You were wise to refuse me."

This admission played like a gong through Bronwyn's heart. He *didn't* despise her. He no longer believed she'd married Ari for money.

What was more, this Patrick was a far cry from the man whose proposal of marriage she'd refused so long ago.

Yes, she could tell Wesley the truth, that Patrick was his father. Wesley would be angry with her, but he deserved the truth. And Patrick deserved that his son knew him.

"So?" he repeated. "When are we going to tell Wesley that I'm his father?"

It happened then. Bronwyn stared past Patrick to the person who'd appeared in the doorway of the fitness room.

Their son.

"Wesley," she snapped, "what are you doing?"

"What did that mean?" he said.

"What did what mean?" she echoed.

Patrick rolled his eyes and turned to face Wesley. He said, "Wesley, I'm your biological father. Your mother and I knew each other before she met Ari. She was married to him, but carrying my baby—you."

Bronwyn winced. It seemed such a brutal, bare-facts recital. She tried to read Wesley's reaction.

Wesley said, "Oh."

"And if you'll let me," Patrick said, "I plan to always be in your life as your father."

Wesley looked sullen, but he said, "Okay." He glared at his mother. "You weren't going to tell me, were you, Mum?"

"I was," she said. "I just didn't know when or how. I came here because Patrick was here, because I wanted you two to know each other."

"You lied to my— You lied." He seemed to feel he could no longer call Ari his dad.

Patrick caught the slip, the awkwardness. He said, "Wesley, Ari is your father, too. It doesn't hurt me for you to acknowledge that. You loved him, and he was important to you."

"But he abandoned me and my mum."

"He was murdered," Bronwyn said.

"No, when he went to jail, and the police took everything. He didn't provide for us."

Bronwyn felt stunned. She hadn't married Ari so that he would "provide." But since his death, she'd let Wesley know her resentment that they'd been left destitute. And Wesley had begun to think less of Ari because of it.

"Wesley, you and I are both going to have to work at remembering the *good* things he did," she said. "He taught you to ride a bicycle. He used to take us sailing. He practiced soccer with you. He cared about you, and he believed you were his son."

"But I never was. You lied to him. You're as bad as he was." Wesley's eyes suddenly filled with tears. He turned and fled.

"Wesley!" Bronwyn started to go after him, but Patrick gently grasped her arm, stopping her.

"Let him have his privacy. He's angry and confused and in mourning. Let him have some space."

Bronwyn wanted to go to Wesley, to somehow make him see that what she'd done was…what? Right? It hadn't been. Necessary? Not that, either. Easiest?

Too true.

She sank down on the floor and sat back against the wall.

"He's right," she said. "I'm as bad as he was."

Patrick shook his head. He just stood, lost in his own thoughts. Then, he said, "I'm going to check on him. Make sure he's not doing anything crazy."

"Wesley wouldn't. He's levelheaded."

"And right now, he's angry."

Wesley picked up some grapes that had fallen from the kissing gate outside the bungalow and threw them at the house.

"Young man!"

He spun around.

It was Louisa Fairchild.

He was very glad he wasn't crying. "What?" he said.

"What, ma'am," she corrected, "or 'What, Louisa?'"

"What, Louisa?" he said in a flat tone.

"No throwing grapes at buildings or anything else. If you're in a mood, go out to the stable and ask one of the grooms if you can help muck out a stall. We don't behave destructively when we're angry."

"All right." He might as well muck out a stall. He really wasn't Wesley Theodoros. He supposed he was Wesley Davies, which was what he was now called in school. And a man he'd only known for about a month was suddenly his father.

"Why are you angry, by the way?" Louisa said.

Wesley saw Patrick come out of the big house behind her. "He'll tell you," he said. And he turned away and headed for the stables.

After Patrick's brief explanation, Louisa said, "I see. Yes, I can see why he's angry. I told him to go muck out a stall."

"I think I'll join him," Patrick said.

"He's angry at his mother?" Louisa asked.

"Probably he's mad at the world."

"Yes, I can see that." She turned to head toward the house. Then, she glanced back. "You might let him know that there will be some advantages to his new status."

"I don't think that's the answer," Patrick said.

Louisa regarded him carefully. "You don't want to spoil him."

"I don't think he can be spoiled at this point," Patrick replied. "Losing people you love tends to drive home just what's important and what isn't."

Louisa nodded. "You'll do, Patrick."

"What do you mean?"

"Well, you're the boy's father, and I think you'll do a fine job at it."

Patrick felt as though no one had ever praised him before. He only wished that Bronwyn felt as Louisa did. "Thank you." He looked toward the stables. "So, we'll see how this goes."

Patrick grabbed a pitchfork and joined Wesley in the empty stall he was cleaning. He said, "I'll leave if you want. I thought you might want company."

Wesley shrugged, apparently indifferent even to Beckham, who had just found his master and was being ignored.

"Out of the way, Beckham," was all Wesley said.

"I hope you can forgive your mother, Wesley."

"Well, I can't, so don't bother mentioning it. She's ruined my life."

Patrick tried not to smile at the sweeping statement. "How do you work that out?"

"I'm no one. I've thought my whole life I was Ari Theodoros's son. It turns out I wasn't. And I wasn't your son, either, because you didn't know, did you?"

"No. I didn't know. Maybe you should focus on the now. I'm *glad* you're my son, and I hope you don't feel that the fact of being my son is going to ruin your life."

"I'm illegitimate. A bastard. That's what it's called."

"Actually, that's impossible. Your mother was married at the time you were born, and Ari is listed on your birth certificate. So neither of those things are true. But if they were, I wouldn't be one iota less proud of you. I can't tell you how happy I was when I learned that you're my son. I wasn't pleased that your mother had kept it from me. But I'd already decided you were a very fine boy, and now I'm simply very proud of you."

"She's just like him."

"She's not, Wesley. I'm sure your mum thought she was acting for the best. She might have been disappointed when she found out you weren't Ari's son and maybe she didn't know what to do."

"I don't even want to know when *that* was."

"And when she found out, I'm sure that your welfare was the first thing on her mind. That's why she didn't want to tell you even now. She was frightened."

"Frightened I'd see that she's a liar."

Patrick thought there was probably some truth in this and chose not to argue the point. He said again, "I hope you can forgive her."

"Just like I'm supposed to forgive my— forgive Ari."

"You know," Patrick said, "we don't forgive for other people. We forgive for ourselves, for our own well-being."

Wesley eyed him curiously.

"And it's not easy," Patrick said, thinking he still had trouble forgiving Bronwyn for choosing Ari over him. I should take my own advice, he thought. But perhaps his hurt had taught him what he was now able to impart to Wesley. "When we don't forgive, it eats us up inside. Then, we make decisions that are bad for us. Bitterness just makes a person unhappy. At first, you feel self-righteous, satisfied with what a great person you are in comparison to the person who has hurt you. But that's not real happiness. Real happiness comes from realizing that you make mistakes, too."

"I wouldn't lie like she did," Wesley stated with certainty.

"I hope you're right," Patrick said. "It's certainly a noble goal not to lie. And I try never to lie, and I'm sure your mum feels the same. But your mother was in a tough situation. Perhaps telling your father—" he looked at Wesley as he said this "—would have been more comfortable for her. But she had to think about how it would affect other people."

"It's still lying," Wesley said.

Patrick decided not to champion Bronwyn's cause further at the moment. He had mixed feelings about what she'd done and knew she did, as well.

So he worked silently beside Wesley, and when they'd finished the stall, Wesley said, "I better go feed Beckham now."

"Good idea," Patrick replied.

Wesley paused for a moment. "What should I call you?"

"Whatever you feel comfortable calling me. I imagine you called Ari 'Dad,' so maybe you don't want to call me that."

Wesley shrugged. "Maybe."

"I want you to do what feels most natural to you," Patrick told him.

"Okay," Wesley said. "Come on, Beckham."

Patrick was glad to find Bronwyn on the porch of the bungalow that night. The rest of the building was dark.

"Is Wesley asleep?" he asked, sitting down on the top step.

"Yes. I just looked in on him."

"Everything okay?"

Bronwyn made a noncommittal gesture.

"You think the time might be ripe for the two of you to move into the big house? It would make things easier for Louisa."

"Why?"

"She has just hired a female groom who would love the chance to live here. You and Wesley are taking up two rooms in the cottage."

"Well, that's difficult to argue with," Bronwyn said.

"I thought you might feel that way. Feel like a walk?"

"A short one—and not too far from the house. Marie and Helena are asleep, too, I think, but if Wesley wakes up he'll come looking for me. I don't like to leave him."

"I know," Patrick said with a faint smile.

"What does that mean?"

"That you're a good mum."

They headed down to the stables, walking through the darkened building, soothed by the familiar smells and sounds of horses.

Bronwyn felt Patrick's hand on her shoulder, and she turned. "What?"

He dropped his hand. "May I kiss you?"

She wanted him to kiss her. That was the simple answer. "Do you think that's a good idea?"

"I think it's a *great* idea," he said cheerfully.

That made her laugh. "Oh, well, then."

He did kiss her, and she liked the taste and smell of him. She found herself kissing not just his mouth, but his chin and his jaw, his cheekbones, all the planes of his face. And she was being kissed with even greater tenderness in return.

There was not just physical excitement there. He seemed to be concentrating with every fiber of his being.

Bronwyn disengaged herself from him slowly and gently.

She felt him watching her questioningly, as though measuring her response. "What?" she said.

"Was that all right?"

"What do you think?"

"You were responsive."

"Yes," she agreed.

She moved closer to the nearest stall. In the moonlight, she could see the occupant, a handsome Thoroughbred. "It's An Indecent Proposal, isn't it?"

"No. If I'd invited you to lie down in the straw..." Patrick teased, a smile in his voice.

"You know what I mean."

"Yes. Handsome bugger, isn't he?" He took Bronwyn's hand, and they walked down the center aisle of the stable, pausing to look at one horse or another, until they came to an empty stall. "Louisa had Wesley clean this today."

"Why?" Bronwyn stepped inside, glancing around.

"He was angry. She thought it was a good way to channel his anger."

"I can't disagree," Bronwyn remarked. "Better to work than—well, other things." She added, "I like her so much Patrick. Your great-aunt."

"She inspires love, doesn't she? Even initially, when

I came here full of prejudice against her, I found myself caring about her."

There was a sound from the far end of the stable, a human sound.

Patrick pulled Bronwyn back against the side of the stall. He peered toward the darkened aisle, then slunk down near Bronwyn.

She looked at him questioningly, but he shook his head.

Together, they waited in the shadows, listening to the sound of slow footsteps.

Occasionally, Patrick risked another look at whoever had entered the stable.

Bronwyn wondered at his insistence on silence. Finally, the person seemed to have had enough of the stables, and she heard the light footsteps receding, heard the person leave the building.

"What?" she whispered.

Patrick glanced out again. In an undertone, he said, "Marie Lafayette. I wonder what she was up to."

"Visiting the horses, I should imagine," Bronwyn replied.

"I wonder." Patrick led her out of the stalls.

"You wonder what?" Bronwyn demanded. "Marie's all right."

He simply glanced at her.

"Did you see her do something?" Bronwyn felt defensive for her friend.

"No, I didn't. But I'm not sure I trust her."

"Well, I do."

"Yes, you're known throughout the continent for your discernment."

A reference to Ari. "That was low."

"I suppose it was. But I'm fairly certain Marie Lafayette is hiding something."

"Like what?"

"I don't know. There was a small irregularity with her paperwork. I don't suppose she's told you much about her background."

"I haven't asked her. I like her. She's a decent woman."

"She's savvy is what she is," Patrick remarked.

"Since when is that a crime?"

"Bronwyn, just consider the possibility that you're being naive."

She did. Then dismissed it. "She's a good person. I know because of her behavior, decisions she makes. I like her."

"*Liking* someone isn't enough, Bronwyn. Try to develop some healthy skepticism."

"I trust my instincts," she replied tartly.

Instead of the rebuttal she expected, he smiled down at her, perhaps remembering the recent intimacy of their kiss. "Then I hope your instincts are right," he conceded. "Let's get you back to our son."

The following day, Bronwyn and Wesley moved into the big house. The assistant housekeeper gave them the same rooms they'd occupied during their initial stay in the house and added that Miss Fairchild would be expecting them to join her for meals.

Bronwyn replied that they would be pleased to do so.

Agnes turned to Wesley, "I understand that you are Miss Fairchild's great-great-nephew, Master Wesley."

"Yes, ma'am," Wesley said with dignity. He didn't meet his mother's eyes, but he was certainly cooperating, and Bronwyn wondered if he was feeling more forgiving toward her than he had the day before.

As Bronwyn began to unpack in her room, Wesley came in. "Mum."

"Yes?" She turned to him, then, seeing his expression, sat down on the edge of the bed. "What is it?"

"Could I change my name to Wesley Stafford? Could I be called that?"

A thousand objections went through Bronwyn's mind. All were based on fear—fear that this would be the first step in losing Wesley to Patrick.

But she had no reason to fear that. Louisa would not let that happen. And, in any case, Bronwyn no longer believed that Patrick would be spiteful toward her. Rather, she'd begun to see him as a good friend—and as someone with whom she could share the responsibility of parenting Wesley.

She pointed out, "Patrick and I aren't married."

"But that doesn't matter," Wesley said. "He says I'm his son."

"Yes, but—" Bronwyn hunted for an objection which would make sense to her son. "I mean, I'm sure Patrick is proud you're his son, but you've always lived with me, so I think you should still have my last name. Has Patrick suggested this?"

Wesley shrugged, looking uncomfortable.

Bronwyn's hackles went up. "Has he?" she repeated.

"It kind of came up," Wesley said, which made her wonder whether her son was protecting Patrick or himself.

"How did it come up?"

"Mum, everybody knows you were married to Ari. Everyone at school. Now they want to know why I have your last name."

Bronwyn began to see the problems this presented for Wesley. "Do you mean they think you're illegitimate? You're not."

"People just want to know why I have my mum's last name. They think it's weird. And I feel stupid telling them I'm Patrick's son if I don't have his last name."

"So you haven't told them," Bronwyn surmised.

Wesley shook his head, looking depressed.

Bronwyn swallowed her own fear. "Let Patrick and me talk about this, okay?"

"Why can't I choose?"

"Maybe you can. But we're not going to rush."

"I know what I want," Wesley said.

"I don't doubt it. Nonetheless, your father and I will make this decision. Together."

"You don't care what life is like for me. You never care." Bursting into tears, Wesley ran from the room. She heard his door shut. Not slam, but shut.

Damn it. Everything seemed to be conspiring to make her look like Medea—to her child, no less.

Chapter Ten

Unfortunately, the next time Bronwyn saw Patrick was in her yoga class that evening. She corrected a couple of his postures with rather more aloofness than she showed the other students. She didn't know what else to do, because she couldn't touch him without remembering kissing him in the barn—or thinking what it would be like to do more, to make love with him again.

Then she would remember that Wesley wanted to take Patrick's last name, and she knew she and Patrick had to discuss that. She felt almost as though an invisible web was stringing itself around her, drawing her closer to Patrick, drawing her into a relationship. It would be so easy, and it wasn't what she wanted. She needed her independence, needed to explore the person she was now, free of Ari. She was growing; life had never been so satisfying or exciting, and the thought of anything hemming her in frightened her.

The grooms had begun to trickle back into this evening yoga class, all of them keen to increase flexibility and correct any alignment problems. They were all strong athletes. Their jobs included riding the horses in the morning gallops, an experience Bronwyn did not envy them. She liked to watch the horses, but had no desire to ride animals as spirited as any of the racehorses.

The name change continued to nag at her as she worked. She must protect both her own interests and Wesley's. She ought to talk to an attorney. She hadn't yet engaged one and was highly reluctant to approach Louisa and ask her to make good on her promise. It flew in the face of her independent nature to rely on an elderly woman and her money.

But she'd promised Wesley that she would speak to Patrick about his name, and so she must.

Patrick lingered after class, as she'd suspected he would.

With a deep sigh, she turned to him. "Wesley has told me he wants to change his last name to Stafford. Did that idea come from you?"

"Yes. I thought it would be a comfort to him."

"You didn't think it might be wise to run the idea past *me* before suggesting it to him?"

"Actually, as soon as it was out of my mouth. I *should* have spoken to you first. And I'm sorry."

She felt all the impotence of someone who was angry and discovered she had no reason to be angry. "He'll never let me rest until he gets his own way on this. You know how painful the situation is for him with Ari. He's entered school with my maiden name, and now he's got all kinds of sensitivities about that, too."

"You can't lay that at my feet."

"And you and I aren't married. Now, if he changes his name to Stafford, people will see me as the unwed mother and also assume that Wesley's bond to you is closer than his bond to me."

"Does it really matter what people think?"

"It matters to me, and it obviously does to Wesley."

"Then, I have a solution, one anyone would agree is in Wesley's best interest."

"Yes?"

He wiped a towel across his face and eyed her blandly. "We could marry."

Bronwyn didn't know what to say. "That would be entirely inappropriate."

He laughed. "Why?"

"I mean— I don't want to be married. I don't want to depend on anyone but me."

"We all depend on other people, Bronwyn. It's how we get through life."

"Yes, but I need to earn my way. That's all."

"And marrying me would interfere with that? You think I'm going to keep you barefoot, pregnant and in the kitchen?"

The idea made her laugh, too—at herself. Then she remembered how she'd hurt him long ago and suddenly understood what courage it must have taken for him to propose marriage once again, whether for Wesley...or because he cared for her.

She laid a hand on his arm. "It's not you. If I wanted to marry anyone, it would be you—"

"It would?" He looked ridiculously pleased by the possibility.

"But I need my independence right now. I need space to...well...*bloom.*"

"I hear you," he said. "But it still might be best for Wesley."

Bronwyn considered and saw just how susceptible she was to the picture of Patrick, Wesley and her as a family. Wasn't some shadowy image of that the reason she had come to Fairchild Acres?

No, she protested stubbornly. She'd just wanted Wesley to know his father.

But that wasn't all. Growing up on the streets with only her mother, never knowing her own father, she had been anxious for a steady male presence in Wesley's life.

"Let's not rush into anything," she said. "Please."

"Does that mean you don't want Wesley changing his last name to Stafford?"

"Not now. Maybe…later. He didn't even know you a month ago."

"Don't you think sooner might be better than later?"

"Why are you pushing me on this?" she asked. "Do you have some motive? Changing his last name is not going to magically make his life better."

Someone cleared her throat, and both turned to see Louisa standing in the doorway of the fitness center, leaning on her cane.

She lifted her eyebrows, indicating that she had heard at least Bronwyn's last words. But what she said was, "Bronwyn, you had a call, and it seemed important, but you were teaching. These people have been trying to find you. I think they finally found you because of that newspaper article."

Bronwyn took the piece of paper the older woman held out. Attorney. Craig Scott. "Thank you, Louisa. He's not at the office now, is he?"

"That's a home number. He seemed very keen to speak with you."

"He didn't say what it was about?"

"I don't think he could. And perhaps you and I should talk, Bronwyn," Louisa added pointedly. "I have some names to give you of attorneys who specialize in divorce and paternity law." Louisa shot a cool look at her great-nephew.

"You misunderstood Bronwyn," Patrick said.

"How so?"

Bronwyn put her hands on her hips. "Don't do this to Louisa, Patrick. It's not remotely fair."

"I'm not trying to take Wesley away from you," he told Bronwyn, then turned to his great-aunt. "Wesley is uncomfortable with the dual stigma of being the son of Ari Theodoros and bearing his mother's last name. I suggested a solution which addressed both. He could take the last name Stafford. He likes the idea."

"Get out," Louisa said.

"What?"

"Get off this property. I told you I wouldn't countenance this."

"I've asked Bronwyn to marry me," Patrick said. "I don't deserve these accusations. I've spoken highly of Bronwyn to Wesley and tried to show him the advantage of forgiving her for not telling him earlier that I'm his biological father. And I've just apologized to Bronwyn for mentioning the name change to Wesley before discussing it with her."

Louisa hesitated. "Yes. I'm sure Wesley is now going to make his mother's life hell until she goes along with it. And naturally, it will be heartbreaking for him if you were to say that you don't want him to bear your name."

Patrick thought, This isn't fair. He'd made a mistake, and he'd admitted it. Well, now he was going to have to try to rectify it, too. He said, "I'll take care of it."

"How?" Bronwyn asked, as though wondering how anyone could untangle the knot Patrick had made.

"I'll say that you and I aren't ready to commit to each other and that it's perfectly appropriate for him to keep your last name in the meantime. I suggest you also allow him to use the name Theodoros if he prefers that."

"That will make him popular," Louisa interjected.

"But it's a start," Bronwyn said. "Thank you, Patrick. I think if you assure him that you and I both feel this way it will help to placate him."

"Thank you," he said and then looked at his aunt. "Shall I pack?"

She gave her head one small shake then swayed slightly on her feet.

Patrick and Bronwyn both stepped toward her as though to catch her. But Louisa straightened up on her own. "It's my bedtime."

"I'll see you upstairs," Bronwyn said firmly.

Louisa didn't object. The two women left Patrick behind in the fitness room and climbed the stairs together.

Bronwyn's heart felt bound to Louisa's. It wasn't just gratitude for all Louisa had done for her and offered to do. It was gratitude for knowing the older woman, for having the benefit of her wisdom, having the privilege of her friendship. As they made their way up the staircase, she said, "Louisa, thank you so much for having me here. Thank you for being such a friend to me."

"I'm not sure how good a friend I'm being."

"Why?"

They'd reached the top of the steps. Louisa leaned

on her cane and looked at Bronwyn. "Because I see myself in you. A softer woman might be a better model. I'm hard on Patrick. I wouldn't want you to let any man walk all over you, but my own life experiences have made me…sometimes hard on the opposite sex."

"Everyone falls in love," Bronwyn said. "It's a universal human experience." She was fishing. She wanted to know all about Louisa's past, most of all why Louisa had thrown her sister out of Fairchild Acres all those years ago.

"That's certainly true," Louisa agreed. "Some people are more forgiving of betrayal than I am, however. And if there's one thing I detest, it's people who try to separate any child from his mother."

Bronwyn had to be honest. "I don't think Patrick was doing that. I believe that he just made a mistake and spoke without thinking. I do believe he wanted Wesley to be happier. And he's proud of him, too. Of course he wants Wesley to have his name. Who wouldn't?"

Louisa laughed. "Thus speaks a mother. But it happens I entirely agree with you on that score. Wesley's a very fine boy." Two steps later, she added, "You see? I'm suspicious where there's probably no need. And I shouldn't encourage you to be so skeptical. I think you and I together may have a sight too much street sense for feminine softness. That's why I said I'm not sure I'm a good model for you. You may be better off trusting Patrick, trusting that he loves you and Wesley.

And actually, I believe he does. He's a complicated man. I've seen some rough edges, but they all have them, don't they?"

"I think he's head and shoulders above the crowd," Bronwyn admitted. "I care for Patrick. But maybe you can understand how much I need to be independent for a while. Maybe always. I loved Ari, strange as that may sound to you, but I was also bound to him. It never felt like confinement till he was gone. Now, I'm free, and I like it."

Louisa looked thoughtful. "I can't give you advice. And I'm not a woman who will tell you to marry for security or even because you think you're in love. I'd probably tell you to hold on to that freedom till your last breath. The heart is an uncertain instrument, and I never depend upon it. But I'm not sure my way of looking at such things is wise. It may just be cowardly."

Bronwyn accompanied Louisa down the hall to the older woman's room, slowing her steps to match the matriarch's. "I can't picture you as a coward—or think of you that way."

"What else would you call the inability to trust?" Louisa retorted. "Go on and call that attorney. I'll see you in the morning."

"You're feeling all right?"

"Extremely well. I'm going to have some toast before bed."

"Good plan. I'll call Agnes for you," Bronwyn replied, impulsively embracing Louisa.

Patrick's great-aunt looked both startled and pleased.

* * *

"It's about the will of your late husband, Ari Theodoros."

"I thought all Ari's assets had been seized."

"Actually, there was a very legitimate insurance policy, and you are the beneficiary."

Bronwyn's heart pounded, and her fingers clutched the telephone receiver more tightly. She had made the call from the extension in her bedroom. "How much is it?" she asked Craig Scott.

"Five million dollars."

Bronwyn sank down on the bed, unable to speak.

Ari *had* provided for her and Wesley, provided in a very substantial way.

Ari, she thought, oh, Ari, thank you.

No longer would she need to take Louisa's charity. No longer would she have to fear Patrick Stafford's power.

You've already stopped doing that, Bronwyn.

Almost. She still must have some doubt, or she would simply let Wesley change his name as he wanted.

Perhaps Louisa was right about what constituted courage.

And maybe Bronwyn herself should think hard about what constituted freedom.

Louisa, Bronwyn reasoned, was the first who deserved to know of the change in Bronwyn's financial status. Inheriting money could not mean turning her back on Fairchild Acres. She was too involved in the fitness center there. One of the grooms had recently been diagnosed with functional scoliosis. The woman knew she needed to stop riding, but Louisa was willing to keep her on in the capacity of assistant trainer. Bronwyn's job would involve working with the groom on a yoga program designed especially for people with scoliosis. It had been part of her training in her recent seminar in Sydney, and now she hoped to learn more from the teacher she'd studied with that week.

No, her job at Fairchild Acres had begun to feel like a career, and Bronwyn only hoped Louisa would be willing for her to remain now that she'd come into an inheritance. Somehow, she didn't think that would be a problem.

She went up to her room that night to hear Wesley calling for her.

Bronwyn tapped on his door before walking in. "What is it, sweetie?"

"Mum, Patrick said you guys decided I couldn't change my name."

"We decided that we don't want you to change it *now,*" Bronwyn said, "which is a different thing."

"Because you're not married to each other," Wesley said.

Bronwyn hadn't known that Patrick planned to discuss the matter with Wesley so soon. She also immediately felt suspicious that Patrick had chosen to emphasize the fact that they weren't married. She reminded herself of the conversation with Louisa on the subject of trust.

"How do you feel about that?" Bronwyn decided to ask.

"I wish we were more like a normal family."

"Normal how?"

"Oh—that you and Patrick were married to each other and I was your kid."

"You *are* our son."

"But it doesn't really seem like it, does it?" he said.

"What do you mean?"

He shrugged. "I don't know."

Long experience with her son had taught Bronwyn that sometimes answers demanded patience. She needed to be available, to listen until Wesley finally revealed what he wanted to say.

So she waited.

"Is he always going to be around?" Wesley finally asked.

"I think that's his plan," Bronwyn said, biting down a smile.

"So...what is...Ari?"

Bronwyn blinked in the dark, trying to read the meaning behind Wesley's words as she studied his anxious face. "I don't understand."

"I mean, he used to be my father."

"I think you can still consider him your father. Now you have another father, as well."

"What if I don't want to think of him as my father?" Wesley said with a trace of bitterness in his voice.

"Wesley…" Bronwyn hesitated, unsure how to express what she wanted Wesley to know—that Ari *had* cared, that he'd provided for them, that despite his criminal behavior he hadn't been a complete monster. She settled on saying, "Ari loved you. He loved you and he loved me. The fact that he was a criminal doesn't have to change the fact of that love for either of us."

"If he'd loved us, he wouldn't have done it."

Bronwyn gave a rueful laugh.

"What?" Wesley said crossly.

"Nothing is that simple, Wes. It's just not. When someone has a weakness—and Ari obviously had more than one—love for someone else isn't necessarily enough to make him overcome temptation. The decision to do the right thing comes from within a person. It's actually not very nice to expect someone to be good because he loves you. That takes away his freedom to act. Also, it makes his love less of a gift. It says that love isn't love unless it is accompanied by certain agreements."

Wesley seemed to think about this. "But what about when people are married?"

"Commitments between people often have rules attached. But the rules are attached to the commitment, not so much to the love. Love is bigger than all of that."

Wesley was quiet for a time.

"Think you can sleep?" Bronwyn asked.

"Do you think you'll marry Patrick?"

Patrick had proposed marriage to her. Bronwyn hoped he'd at least kept *that* from Wesley. But Wesley hadn't mentioned it, so perhaps Patrick had. Bravo, Patrick, she thought. A modicum of discretion.

"Suppose Patrick and I were to decide we want to marry. How would you feel about it?"

Wesley seemed to consider. "I'd like it. It would be more normal." He frowned. "Why are you smiling?"

"When you're older, I think you'll put less value on what other people decide is 'normal.'"

Wesley was quiet. "Maybe."

Bronwyn kissed him, said good-night again and stepped out into the hall.

Patrick saw her emerge from Wesley's room.

Walking quietly, he started toward her, and she met him halfway.

"Let's go in the office," he suggested. His office. Inside, he shut the door. "A nightcap?"

"Thank you."

He poured them each a glass of cognac, handed Bronwyn's to her. "Cheers."

They drank.

Bronwyn resisted the urge to pick a fight with him by saying that he hadn't needed to tell Wesley that the name change was somehow dependent on Patrick's and Bronwyn's marrying. What did it matter what he'd told Wesley? What mattered was that Wesley was now nurturing hopes that his mother and father might end up together.

We could, Bronwyn thought. For Wesley.

But she couldn't bear to think of marrying for that reason. She felt as though bands were constricting her, trying to imprison her.

"Did I make things better?" he asked.

"Yes." Wesley seemed to accept that his own wishes wouldn't be the sole factor in whether or not he was allowed to change his name. "Thank you," she added.

"I wanted to ask you," Patrick said, "if you'd fly to London with me in February. Just the two of us. Wesley will be busy in school, and Megan has said she would watch him."

"That's a long way off," Bronwyn said.

"Which is why I wanted to tell you as soon as possible—to give you time to consider."

"Ah." She sipped her drink. "Why just me?"

Patrick joined her beside the window where she stood. He removed her glass from her hands, set it next to his on the highboy. "Because I'm attracted to you. Because once you were my best friend. Because I've never found another woman who compares to you."

"And because I'm the mother of your child," she added.

He gave a rueful laugh. "That has less to do with it…if I'm honest with myself."

"What do you mean?"

"I'm *glad* that you and I have a child together. But that wouldn't be enough to make me love you."

To make me love you. Was he saying that he *did* love her? Bronwyn wondered.

"What I want to know," he said, touching a lock of the long hair that now hung loose on each side of her face, "is if you love me, too."

Bronwyn spoke quietly. "I do. But—"

He cocked an eyebrow.

"I need to be free, Patrick. It all seems so easy, to become your lover, your wife. But it's too easy. I'm not sure I want…" The right words eluded her. "I've inherited money from Ari. His life insurance."

Patrick half opened his mouth. Abruptly, he closed it. "What will you do?"

"Nothing different, at the moment."

He nodded, thinking, then gazed at her from those hazel eyes, and she stared at his mouth, at the dent in his chin.

"Does being free," he asked, "mean you can't love me?"

She met his eyes. "Patrick, lately I can't help loving you."

He reached for her again, slowly, tentatively, as though determined to make no mistake.

She lifted her face to his.

Chapter Eleven

They spent the night in Patrick's bedroom, and Bronwyn could not deny the comfort, the *rightness* of being so intimate with him. As she lay in his arms, her thoughts spun from a past almost forgotten to the present. The lover who embraced her now was both steadier and deeper than her boyfriend from university. And she was in love with him, joyful to be close to him.

Yes, Patrick had changed. And so had she. Ruefully, she thought of the early years of her marriage, of coming to terms with the fact that Patrick was Wesley's biological father, of her decision to continue letting Ari believe Wesley was his son.

Yes, she'd grown. All the emotional growth in her

life seemed so hard-won. It had always been that way. And now she seemed to have all she wanted. A career, money of her own, family, Patrick's love.

Experience, however, had made her distrustful of such situations, scenarios in which she had all she wanted. To have everything she wanted was to be vulnerable.

In her vulnerability, the person she most wanted to distrust was Patrick.

Trust equals courage, she thought, remembering all the things Louisa had said that evening. Patrick had shown himself to be a person who could listen to her, who could admit to weakness in himself. They could grow together.

"Do you think it will be all right with Louisa if I continue to live here and teach here?"

"I don't think it would be all right if you left," Patrick replied. "You're family to her."

Bronwyn propped herself up on her elbows. The moon was almost full, and its silvery light came through the window. She gazed at Patrick. "It's hard for me to take in. The only family I've ever had was my mum. Then Ari and Wesley."

"I want you to be part of my family, Bronwyn. I want you for my wife."

"I can't," she said quickly. "I've told you why."

Patrick only heard her rejection, an echo of earlier rejection. This woman had never said to him that he was someone she could marry, only that she wouldn't marry him. And she had married someone else. He tried to remember the reason she'd given for not marrying him—for not marrying him now. "In the past," he said, "you felt that I was immature and unready for marriage. Is that how you still feel?"

"Absolutely not. I admire you. I even love you. I'm glad you're Wesley's father. If I were to marry anyone now, I would want it to be you."

"But," he said.

"I've been widowed a very short time, Patrick. Can't you understand my wanting to figure out who I am before linking my life to someone else's?"

"Are you asking me to wait?"

"I would never ask any man to wait," she said sharply. But his words troubled her. "Are you saying you're simply looking for a wife and if I don't want to marry you, then you need to find someone else?"

"I'm not saying that," he told her, holding her more tightly. "I was trying to get a feeling—to find out if you think you could marry me in the future."

"If I can marry anyone in the future," Bronwyn said, "it would be you. Can't you see that it's much too soon for me?"

He thought about it, about the turmoil which had brought her to Fairchild Acres. He tried to believe her, to believe that this rejection was not like the last. But it was still rejection, and his whole body ached with it. He stroked her head and said, "I understand."

Because he did. But he also understood that this Bronwyn, freed from her life with Ari Theodoros, might never want to marry again.

And Patrick could see that he might have become the right man for her.

But that it might be too late.

It was 5:30 a.m. Wesley was not yet awake. Patrick had followed Bronwyn into her room, where she was dressing to teach a six o'clock spinning class. Helena and Marie were her most faithful students for indoor cycling. Helena had lost fifteen pounds since Bronwyn had come to Fairchild Acres, and the weight loss was accompanied by an increase in muscle tone. Bronwyn couldn't have been more pleased with her friend's progress.

As she finished lacing her trainers, Patrick asked, "Do you mind if I drive Wesley to school?"

"Don't you think it's best for him to ride the bus?"

Patrick narrowed his eyes. "Why?"

Bronwyn shook her head. "I don't want to spoil him."

"It sounds as though Ari spoiled him a bit."

"And it was a problem—for me, anyway. Sometimes I could see Wesley starting to become arrogant because of Ari's wealth. That's not how I want him to be."

"Nor I," Patrick agreed. "Though to be honest, I don't think there's much chance of that. You've done a very fine job with him, Bronwyn."

His words touched her, and she looked at him and

said, "And I think you're wonderful for him. I'm so glad that he knows he's your son. I think he's already taking strength from it, from believing in you."

He gave her a small, wry smile. "I'll try to be worthy." Then he suggested, "I'll walk to the bus stop with him. How will that be?"

"Perfect." Bronwyn kissed him.

He gazed into her green eyes, trying to read the truth there, trying to believe that she loved him more than she could any other man. And trying to accept that, once again, she didn't want to marry him.

That afternoon, she and Patrick walked to the bus stop together to meet Wesley. They planned to go for a ride afterward.

Patrick and Wesley would use their riding horses. Bronwyn would be on Exclusive, an elderly and retired jumper whom she enjoyed riding. Exclusive was housed in the stable that Louisa's most valuable racehorses occupied, while Patrick's and Wesley's were in a different building, so they separated and agreed to meet outside the racing stable.

On the way to the stable, Bronwyn met Crystal, the groom with scoliosis who was no longer participating in the morning gallops. Riding Thoroughbreds was not recommended for her spine.

"How are you, Crystal?" Bronwyn asked.

The twenty-two-year-old, who was black-haired,

tiny enough to be a jockey and very pretty, replied with a slightly bitter smile. "At least I still get to be around the horses."

"You miss riding," Bronwyn said.

"It's all I've ever cared about."

Bronwyn racked her brain, trying to think of something, anything, that would fill the gap where riding Thoroughbreds had been in this young woman's life. "You like dancing?" she asked halfheartedly. "Cycling?"

"Why is cycling okay and riding isn't? No, don't answer that, and I know I can ride now. It's just not the smartest thing. I know I'm making the right choice."

But tears had sprung to her eyes as she spoke.

"Shall we see how great you can get at yoga?" Bronwyn said.

"I do like to dance. But just clubbing, you know. I've never learned a dance discipline."

"What type interests you?" Bronwyn asked.

"Probably modern—to watch. But you have to start with ballet when you're young. I like your yoga classes—and Pilates."

"I'm taking lots of extra training courses," Bronwyn said. "Next time I have to go, why don't you come with me? I think we could use another teacher. You're already an athlete, and that eliminates a lot of hurdles."

"I'd love that," Crystal said. She gave an uneasy glance toward the racing stables. "Well, you're going riding, right?"

"Yes. Oh, and here come Patrick and Wesley."

"Patrick fancies you, doesn't he?"

Bronwyn gave a small grin. "A bit, I think." She winked at the other girl. "But I thought it was a closely guarded secret."

"I won't give you away," Crystal laughed. "He's a handsome devil, isn't he?"

"Oh, yes."

Bronwyn waved to Patrick and Wesley. "Sorry, you guys. I'll saddle up Exclusive. Give me a moment."

Crystal, instead of waving goodbye, walked over to the other two to compliment Wesley on his riding and talk to him about Beckham, who had walked over to pee on a post by the stable.

Bronwyn spotted Marie walking around the side of the stable, looking as though she'd just come from the other end of the building. She was glancing back at her uncle, Reynard. Reynard worked at Lochlain and brought eggs to the kitchen regularly. Bronwyn had always found him charming, but now he and Marie appeared to be arguing, and then Marie stalked away.

She walked to the main stable door and opened it.

A horse's thunderous snorting made her jump. A giant stallion reared before her, untethered, unaccompanied, and charged out of the stable. Bronwyn heard more snorting, hooves rising and falling, a high wail that pierced her brain. She spun to see Wesley fly through the air, thrown by his mount. He struck his head on the edge of a fence and hit the ground like a sack, un-moving.

Bronwyn ran toward him, a voiceless scream inside her.

Patrick yelled, "Don't move him," as he wheeled his horse to go after the stallion.

"No!" Crystal said. "I'll get him, he knows me."

Bronwyn knew the groom must be talking about the horse.

"Grab that horse!" yelled a voice from far away, a voice Bronwyn recognized as Louisa's.

Bronwyn raced over to Wesley, but Marie was already at his side. She touched Wesley's neck at the carotid artery. "He's got a pulse."

"He's breathing," Bronwyn said. "God, call an ambulance. Please, call someone."

Marie ran off to find a phone.

Wesley's eyes fluttered.

"Honey, don't move," Bronwyn said. His neck. Had he hurt his neck? And his head?

Raised voices were still calling to each other about the horse.

"An Indecent Proposal," muttered a voice beside Bronwyn. It was Reynard. He gazed down at Wesley, eyes concerned.

Bronwyn said, "Wesley, hold very still. Can you do that for me?"

"Mum?"

"Don't move, Wesley. You're going to be okay," she

said, praying. How on earth had An Indecent Proposal gotten out of his stall? Bronwyn couldn't imagine any groom at Fairchild Acres being so careless.

"He's out on the highway," said Reynard. "Is your boy all right?" He crouched down beside her.

Another voice asked, "Bronwyn, is he okay?"

Helena.

"Marie sent me out."

Again Wesley said, "Mum."

"Yes, sweetie. Don't move. Please don't move, Wesley. Your horse threw you, and we've called an ambulance, just to make sure you're one hundred percent. How do you feel?"

"Head hurts."

"Don't move," Bronwyn said again, fiercely. She knew how to stabilize an injured neck. It was one of the things she'd learned in first aid and CPR classes at university. "Honey, try not to move a muscle. I'm going to come around behind you, and I'm going to hold your head very tight. This is just in case you've had a spinal injury. That's why it's very important for you not to move. You know that, don't you?"

His eyes, in a face so like Patrick's, watched her solemnly. "Yes, Mummy."

Helena knelt on the dirt beside them. Beckham sniffed around, tried to lick Wesley's face, and Reynard grabbed the dog.

"Thank you," Bronwyn said. "Please hold him.

Helena, you can help me hold Wesley. I'll tell you what to do."

She had several minutes to think of the fragility of the human head as she held Wesley before she heard the siren.

Almost at the same moment, she became aware of an uneven, slow gait, accompanied by the sound of Louisa's cane.

"Oh, my God," Louisa said. "My God. How did that horse get out?"

"Wesley's all right," Bronwyn said, not because she knew it was true, but to soothe the older woman. "I'm just taking precautions." She made herself ask, "Did someone catch the horse?"

"Crystal and Terry."

Terry. Another of the grooms.

"They're walking him, cooling him down," Louisa said. She didn't apologize for checking on the horse first, but Bronwyn wasn't surprised. She'd expected Louisa to be distraught about the stallion.

But Louisa exclaimed, "I'm going to find out who did this. My great-great nephew could have been killed!"

Helena looked up sharply. Despite the gossip at Fairchild Acres, Wesley's relationship to Louisa was news to her. Only Wesley, Patrick, Bronwyn and Louisa had known the truth, and none of them had spoken of it to anyone else, except for Bronwyn, who had confided in Marie.

Reynard cleared his throat. "So that's who he is."

Bronwyn kept her eyes on Wesley's face, annoyed at Reynard for speaking about Wesley as though he wasn't present, upset because she'd felt her son try to turn his head to look at the man who was holding Beckham's collar.

Louisa said, "Reynard, please take Beckham to his dog trolley."

The dog trolley was a temporary containment solution for Beckham. His leash was attached to a roller on a cable overhead, so he could be tied and yet have the freedom to run back and forth. Louisa wanted to make a fenced yard for the dog, but she and Patrick hadn't yet decided the best place for it.

Louisa tried to stoop down to the ground to be nearer Wesley.

"Don't, Louisa," Bronwyn said. "Don't. Look, the ambulance is here. They'll look after Wesley."

Patrick drove Bronwyn to the hospital, and Louisa insisted on accompanying them, "An Indecent Proposal be damned," which of course she hadn't meant. The ambulance had gone ahead of them, and when they arrived they found that Wesley was already in X-ray.

Patrick hadn't spoken a word to Bronwyn since the accident.

While they waited, Louisa repeated, "When I find out why An Indecent Proposal was out—"

"I don't think it was a mistake," Patrick said.

"What do you mean?" Louisa asked, though from the expression on her face, Bronwyn could tell that the old woman had known exactly what Patrick meant.

"I mean it was sabotage," Patrick said. "He's winning. Somebody wanted him to get out, was hoping he'd come to grief, and I have a good idea who."

Louisa lifted her eyebrows.

"Marie Lafayette was coming out of the stables just before Bronwyn opened the doors."

"You don't know that," Bronwyn said. "It looked that way, but I didn't see her come out. I just saw her talking to Reynard. Patrick, no one at Fairchild Acres would intentionally let that horse out. An Indecent Proposal is Louisa's best prospect now, but he isn't the only horse in the stables. And Marie wouldn't let a horse out, Patrick. You don't know her at all."

"And you're easily deceived," Patrick told her.

Irritated by the reference to Ari—Bronwyn could see it no other way—she turned from him, just as a physician in scrubs entered the waiting area.

She stepped toward him.

"I'm Dr. Mosely," he said. "Are you Wesley's mother?"

"Bronwyn Davies. And this is Patrick Stafford, his father, and Louisa Fairchild, Patrick's aunt," Bronwyn fired off rapidly. "What did you find?"

"No spinal cord injury, no broken bones. He has a concussion, and I'm going to let you take him home.

You'll want to wake him up every two hours, make sure he's okay, knows things he should know. We have a care sheet—things to look for. But I don't think you'll have any trouble. He hit his head, but it's a mild concussion."

Bronwyn, Patrick and Louisa all sighed in chorus. Then they looked at each other, and all three laughed. The physician gave an understanding smile. "Why don't you come back and see Wesley. We have some paperwork for you, and we'll let you get on your way."

They were back at Fairchild Acres, where An Indecent Proposal was safely in his stall, before the subject of the horse's escape came up again.

Bronwyn fixed a snack for Wesley, and he and Beckham went up to his bedroom to "try to read," but Bronwyn knew her son was sleepy. Then, Bronwyn joined Patrick and Louisa in the living room, where they were each having a glass of wine before dinner. Patrick poured Bronwyn a glass, too, turning to Louisa as he did so. "She's hiding something, Louisa. I know it."

"Not Marie again," Bronwyn said. "Patrick, I'm telling you, you're wrong."

"How do you know?" he asked.

"She's my friend, and I wouldn't believe she'd do such a thing unless I saw it with my own eyes."

"Maybe not even then," he replied.

Ari. She hated to hear it, hated that she felt complicit

in her husband's crimes, complicit because at some point she'd realized that something was amiss, and yet she'd done nothing.

Louisa said, "Thank you, both of you, for sharing your thoughts on this. I, too, believe the girl has her secrets. But we can't know that her secrets are sinister." She gave a small, tight sigh. "I'd certainly like to know, however."

"I know," Bronwyn said softly.

"You like her," Patrick said. "We've both heard you."

Louisa admitted, "The world of racing has always attracted an unusual breed. Frequently I hire someone knowing he—or she—has a troubling past. Sometimes I know the details. Sometimes I don't. But we are, none of us, without our pasts."

Amen, Bronwyn wanted to say.

"You can learn from a person's past actions," Patrick said.

"Was that directed at me?" Bronwyn asked.

He spun his head, looking mystified. "What are you talking about?"

"You think that because I didn't know what Ari was doing, I'm incapable of judging Marie's character."

"I wasn't thinking about you at all, Bronwyn. This isn't about you or Ari Theodoros. It's about something going on right now at Fairchild Acres. I meant that I would like to know more about Marie's past. Not to mention that uncle of hers."

Louisa interrupted. "A person's past actions are like a snake's skin that has been shed. Yes, they came from the snake, but they aren't the snake. What's more, the snake, since shedding its skin, has become something new and different."

"I like that analogy," Bronwyn said. She knew she would think of her different pasts—homeless on the streets, a student in love with Patrick, a woman choosing Ari, his wife—as various sheddings of her own skin. But now she was someone new. She had changed.

Patrick, however, said, "I agree that you've chosen a good analogy, Louisa. Because no matter how many times a snake sheds its skin, it remains a snake."

Chapter Twelve

"I need to check on Wesley every couple of hours," Bronwyn said later that evening, when Patrick asked if she would like to join him in his room. "I'll just lie down in my room so I'll be closer to him."

"This is about Marie, isn't it?" he said.

"No," she replied truthfully.

He lifted his eyebrows, inviting her to say more.

She lowered her voice to make sure they wouldn't be overheard. "Patrick, you asked me to marry you, and I said no. I love you, and I don't want to do any-thing…dishonest…with you."

"Being my lover is dishonest?"

She shook her head. "I need to slow this all down. I like my life now, and I don't want it to change."

Patrick smiled gently. "I think you can count on life changing, whether you make love with me again or not."

She touched his arm, loving him.

"In any case," Patrick said, abruptly changing the subject, "I hope you won't discourage Louisa from trying to find out more about Marie. I know Marie has been a friend to you. But that doesn't make her harmless, Bronwyn."

"Patrick, I *know* her. I'm not naive. I've lived on the streets, and I trust my instincts."

"What did your instincts tell you about Ari?"

"See!" she exclaimed. "You are dredging that up."

Patrick shook his head. "I'm sorry. That was cheap. Look, since you two are friends, you might ask Marie what she was doing around the stable before An Indecent Proposal got out."

"I'm not going to accuse her of letting that damned racehorse out of his stall. Wesley got hurt, but how that horse got out is nothing to do with me. I'm not a groom. I have nothing to do with the stables."

His jaw was stiff, his expression hiding something. Anxiety perhaps?

"Patrick, Ari used to like to choose my friends. Now I think it was a way of controlling me. But I've made good friends here at Fairchild Acres. Marie and Helena matter to me. I won't turn my back on a friend just because you don't trust her—without reason, I might add."

"I haven't asked you to turn your back on her."

"What do you have against Marie?" Bronwyn repeated.

He sighed, seemed to be debating with himself. "She's furtive, Bronwyn. She's here for a reason, and she hasn't told anyone that reason."

"Like me, coming here to find you? Mightn't it be something as innocuous as that, Patrick?"

She watched his face, watched him thinking. At last he shrugged. "Maybe you and Louisa are right. I'm riled because of what happened to Wesley. Bronwyn, I've never been that scared."

Bronwyn nodded. "Me, either. It's the first time I've ever seen him really get hurt like that."

He reached for her, giving her a long, comforting hug. "Sure you won't change your mind about where you're spending the night?"

She lifted her face and kissed his lips. "Slow," she said.

He touched her cheek gently. "I've always liked your strength, your independence. It's to your credit that you're standing up for a woman you like, Bronwyn."

"Thank you for saying that."

"I mean it. I don't want to control you, God forbid, or pick your friends. I just…"

She studied him.

He never finished the sentence, just gave her a last swift kiss and turned away before she could say another word.

* * *

Patrick lay awake. He *did* know. He knew why he lashed out. He knew why he wanted Bronwyn to take his part.

She didn't love him enough.

Or rather, he didn't believe that her love was as strong and real as his for her.

Why?

Because so many years ago she'd picked Ari. Because she'd pushed him away her first weeks at Fairchild Acres. Because she *did* stand up for herself. Because she was wise enough to see the benefits for Wesley in having his parents married to one another— but also wise enough to want to move slowly. The sum: Patrick was insecure in her love, and he longed for proof that she loved him as deeply as he loved her.

Also, she was wrong about Marie Lafayette. Yes, it was possible that her reasons for being at Fairchild Acres were benign. But if so, why keep her purpose secret? Too much was currently unsettled in the world of Thoroughbred racing. The election, with that sleazy Jacko Bullock running for the ITRF presidency. Sam Whittleson's murder. And last year in Kentucky, a discrepancy in the DNA registry of champion Thoroughbred Leopold's Legacy was linked to an international organization involved in breeding fraud.

Not to mention the chaos and lack of trust caused by the shenanigans of Ari Theodoros. The syndicate was still too involved in the racing world for Patrick's taste, and who was to say that Marie Lafayette wasn't part of their schemes, placed at Fairchild Acres to damage Louisa's stable?

He rolled over, smelling the pillow beside him, which still held the scent of Bronwyn. He couldn't lose her. Yet she seemed more afraid of making herself his.

Uncomfortable with that train of thought, he turned back to Marie. Maybe he would ask Dylan Hastings to look into her background. Yes, why not?

Now, he should be able to sleep.

Right, Patrick.

Bronwyn awoke in the morning knowing she had no classes to teach until eleven. Wesley had made it through the night well and begged to be allowed to go to school since a tarantula expert would be visiting. Bronwyn said he might be able to go briefly to see the spiders. In the meantime he should rest, and she would join Marie on her morning bicycle ride. If Crystal was willing, Bronwyn would coax the groom to come with them. Maybe Helena, too.

She dressed quickly in black cycling shorts and a bright yellow jersey—the best protection against sleepy motorists—grabbed her bicycle helmet and gloves, and hurried downstairs. She'd gone with Marie before, borrowing one of Louisa's bicycles. As for Crystal, Bronwyn wheeled a second bicycle from the shed for her, checking to make sure that the tires were good. She oiled the chains of both bikes, made a minor adjustment to the gears of one, then headed for the bungalow.

She found Marie already dressed for her morning ride. "Hey, can I join you?" Bronwyn asked.

There was something awry in the glance Marie slid her way.

Bronwyn frowned.

"Sure you want to?" Marie asked.

"Why wouldn't I?"

"Rumor has it that I let An Indecent Proposal out of his stall."

"Of course you didn't," Bronwyn replied. "Who told you that?"

"Oh, Reynard thinks Patrick suspects me. And seeing that you and Patrick…"

"I don't give a toss what the rumor mill says," Bronwyn assured her. "I know you wouldn't do something like that."

Marie's eyes suddenly appeared wet and she gazed down at her shoes.

Bronwyn crouched beside her. "Marie, what is it?"

"I'm just glad you trust me," Marie said. "Friends, friends you can count on, are the best thing in the world."

"Amen to that," said Helena, emerging from her room, ready for a ride. She had a bicycle of her own, though she'd ridden it little before Bronwyn came to

Fairchild Acres and encouraged her to train. "Hey, Bronwyn. Why aren't you curled up with the luscious man of the house?"

Bronwyn shrugged. "As Marie said…"

"Friends," Helena agreed.

"Speaking of friends, is Crystal around?"

"Out watching the gallops." Marie sighed. "I asked her if she wanted to come with me, but she said she'd be bad company."

"I'll go try to persuade her. I just worked on one of Louisa's bikes for her."

"Actually, Crystal has one of her own. She hasn't ridden since she got the scoliosis diagnosis. She's sort of in the mode of, 'If I can't ride horses, I'm not going to do anything.'"

Bronwyn said, "We'll see about that." With a smile, she headed out to the track where the Thoroughbreds were running to look for Crystal.

It was Patrick who woke Wesley again following instructions in a note from Bronwyn.

"Where's my mum?" Wesley asked.

"Bicycle riding with her girlfriends. Let's go have breakfast with Louisa and see if you're well enough to go see those spiders."

"Okay." Wesley climbed out of bed, found his school uniform where he'd tossed it on a chair, and began to dress.

"Meet you downstairs," Patrick told him and went out, heading down to the breakfast room.

Louisa was already at the table.

"Wesley's just dressing," Patrick said, "and Bronwyn's off bicycle riding with Marie, making her point."

Louisa's head snapped up. "Surely you don't expect her to turn her back on a friend just to suit you?"

Patrick pulled out his chair and sat. "No, Louisa. I don't. I'm just trying to watch out for…everyone."

Unexpectedly, Louisa laughed. "You're a fine man, Patrick. I'm not complaining about my great-nephew."

"Thank you." He decided not to mention to Louisa that he was going to have Dylan Hastings look into Marie's background. Louisa could be protective of her employees, and she might not be keen on his idea. He could ask Dylan to do it quietly, and that would help put Patrick's own misgivings to rest.

Nonetheless, he found himself saying, "Wasn't Dylan interested in some of our employees back when he was working on the Whittleson murder?"

"He was, but his interest was inappropriate, and Robert told him so."

Robert D'Angelo, Louisa's attorney.

"My employees are like family," Louisa said fiercely. "Well—they're like what family is to other people. Though lately, I've come to care for my blood family more than I'd ever thought possible." She gave Patrick a stern look. "You're not thinking of giving Marie any grief, are you?"

"I'm *thinking* of finding out more about how that horse got out. Someone wants to scupper An Indecent Proposal's chances."

Louisa sighed. "Patrick, with all the people who are involved in deceit of different kinds in Thoroughbred racing, you can't believe that Marie Lafayette is the culprit."

"She's Reynard's niece, and he's around here much more than I like. He's not even an employee. He works for Lochlain Racing. He may be using her as leverage to get—" Patrick stopped speaking abruptly because Mrs. Lipton had entered the breakfast room. He'd noticed that the housekeeper seemed to have a lot of tolerance for Reynard, even found him charming. Of course, Lipton herself had worked for Louisa for years; *she* was beyond suspicion.

Louisa said, "I've heard all I want to hear on the subject. I think it's possible that Crystal neglected to fasten his stall after the morning gallops. She's distracted by her health problems. I've questioned her, and she says she follows a detailed routine in securing the stalls. However..."

"She's not riding."

"But she led him back to his stall yesterday morning."

Mrs. Lipton refreshed Louisa's coffee without asking and topped off Patrick's, as well. Patrick knew she wanted to hear what he'd been saying about Reynard.

But eventually, she left the breakfast room, and

Patrick said, "Well?" as though there had been no inter-
ruption.

"I do not suspect sabotage, Patrick. It was an accident, and that concerns me more than paranoid ideas
about a plot against my horse. Accidents result in harm
to both horses and people. We can't have that kind of
mistake, so I've asked our head groom to draw up a
protocol for stabling horses."

"We already have one."

"We're refining it to eliminate mistakes."

Wesley slipped into the room. "Hi, Louisa."

"Good morning, Wesley. How are you today?"

"I'm okay. I want to go to school. We're studying
spiders, and a tarantula expert is bringing tarantulas to
class."

Patrick said, "I'll take you later this morning. You've
had a concussion. A half day of school is the maximum
today. And no running around."

"Do you like spiders?"

Patrick considered. "Well, when they get beyond a
certain size, I prefer them to live in the wilderness."

"I want to have one as a pet," Wesley announced.

Patrick said, "How do you think your mum would
feel about that?"

"I don't think she minds spiders, as long as they're
not real venomous to people. All spiders are venomous," Wesley added with authority. "But not all of
them have venom which makes people sick. The taran-

tula man is bringing tarantulas that whistle. Just when they're mad, though."

"Is he going to make them mad in the classroom?" Patrick asked.

"I don't know. You can come to the presentation. Parents are invited."

"What about great-great-aunts?" Louisa asked.

Wesley tilted his head at her, interested. "Are you afraid of tarantulas?"

"I'll tell you a secret," Patrick stage-whispered to his son. "She's not afraid of *anything.*"

"Except, perhaps, when small boys hit their heads," Louisa agreed.

"Will you come to school with me?" Wesley asked her.

"Of course," she said. "I would like to see giant whistling spiders."

Bronwyn and Marie were alone as Marie hung her bicycle on the hooks in her room in the employee cottage. Marie had seemed sad, withdrawn and frustrated during the entire ride. Crystal and Helena had ridden side by side while Bronwyn and Marie rode ahead.

Now Bronwyn asked, "Marie, whatever it is, do you want to talk about it?"

The blond woman turned to her, the face that was usually so happy now troubled. "I'm not ready, Bronwyn. And it's nothing bad." Moodily, she turned toward her bed, where her uniform T-shirt and jeans were laid out. Pausing, very still, she asked, "Does Louisa love Patrick and Megan?"

Bronwyn couldn't imagine why Marie would ask such a thing, but she answered, "Very much, I think. She values family. God, she loves me, I think, and I'm not even related by blood. And she loves Wesley, is wonderful to him, like a grandmother. I'm so thankful for her presence in all our lives." She hesitated. "Why do you ask?"

Marie shrugged. "Does she suspect me, Bronwyn?"

"Of what?"

"Of letting An Indecent Proposal out of his stall."

"No," Bronwyn replied firmly. She took a breath. "Did you do it, Marie?"

Marie did not lift her head. "No, I didn't. And neither did Reynard. I'm sure that's on everyone's mind, but he wouldn't do that, either. I know he's...unconventional...but he's family."

Bronwyn hesitated, put her hand on Marie's arm. "Marie, let's you and I try to be a kind of family to each other. I think that's how Louisa sees Fairchild Acres anyway. But I feel so close to you and Helena—and sweet Crystal."

Marie turned to her suddenly, threw her arms around her and hugged her. "Thank you."

"And I'm going to see if there's any breakfast left on the table and check how Wesley is doing."

* * *

Bronwyn entered the breakfast room. "Hi," she said, coming to the table and—with decision—kissing first Patrick's head, then Wesley's, then hugging Louisa. "Sorry I'm sweaty."

Louisa said, "I'm glad you're here. Did you know about the exciting school day Wesley has ahead of him?"

"The spiders. Yes. I got a note from the teacher with an invitation." She pulled out a chair across from Wesley and Patrick and beside Louisa. "But, Wesley—no running, no sports."

"You can cancel your exercise class if you like, Bronwyn," Louisa said.

Bronwyn shook her head. "That wouldn't be fair to the faithful who keep showing up."

"More of them all the time," Louisa said. "I hear nothing but good things about you, Bronwyn."

"Thank you." Bronwyn helped herself to granola and yogurt from serving dishes on the table. "By the way, Patrick, your campaign of intimidation against Marie is working. She expected me to turn my back on her, too."

Silence. He lifted his head. "Campaign of intimidation?" he echoed incredulously. "All I've said is that I think she—"

"You've said too much," Bronwyn told him.

Louisa cleared her throat, and Bronwyn glanced at Wesley to see a stricken look on his face.

He doesn't want to see us fight. In fact, Bronwyn could see Wesley's secure world crumbling in the face of her harsh words to his father. She had just ridden bikes with Marie and had sensed the other woman's deep sadness and loneliness. Marie was troubled, and Bronwyn absolutely would not turn her back on her.

Your own life, Bronwyn. Sort out your own life. She'd greeted Patrick with a kiss as a sign of love for him, but now she wondered if she should have done that, if she was taking advantage of his love. Last night, it had crossed her mind that by rejecting his proposal of marriage, she might lose him, lose the position of being the woman he loved.

She couldn't think about that.

And yet, her living situation, hers and Wesley's, was forcing her hand with Patrick, was pushing her toward becoming his wife.

If I ever do cut it off with him, I'm going to lose this home, as well.

And how would it feel to someday see him with another woman?

But was it fair for her to stay here after saying that she wouldn't marry him? He was in love with her.

And she with him.

Which left marrying him as the comfortable option—the option that she didn't want.

"I'm sorry," she said, "for picking a fight at the table.

I apologize to everyone. Tell me more about the spiders, Wesley. Have you ever seen a tarantula?"

She had to tell Louisa how she was feeling, tell her everything. Bronwyn didn't want to burden Louisa, and yet she felt the necessity of being honest with her employer, her supportive friend, about her conflicted feelings.

So she felt relief when, after breakfast, Louisa said, "Shall we do our work with the treadmill now, Bronwyn, before I go to school with Wesley and Patrick?"

Walking on a treadmill was part of Louisa's health regimen.

"Great." It would be a chance to talk. And explain that she might have to leave Fairchild Acres.

Chapter Thirteen

"You would do that to Wesley?" Louisa said, but she didn't sound angry. Worried, perhaps. Troubled.

"Louisa, I don't know what to do, but it seems wrong to marry Patrick just because we're living in the same place and have a child together. And he wants to marry me, and I do love him, so I'm feeling some pressure to agree. But it feels wrong. I need to be sure of the two of us."

Louisa walked steadily on the treadmill, and Bronwyn slowed the machine and touched the older woman's shoulder, making a minor correction in her posture. After a few more minutes on the treadmill, they would switch to the Pilates machines.

"I'm happy here," Bronwyn said. "I don't remember ever being this happy before. But marriage should be a choice, not an accident of timing and circumstance."

Louisa nodded. Then, with an air of conviction she remarked, "If you're willing to risk losing Patrick, I doubt your love *is* strong enough."

The words went to Bronwyn's core.

Was she willing to risk losing Patrick? Lose him again?

Louisa was right. Bronwyn had turned her back on Patrick once before, and even now she wasn't one hundred percent certain he'd forgiven her. But it did seem she'd regained his trust. Could she risk shattering his faith in her?

But my independence, she thought. Can I relinquish that?

"You're very wise," Bronwyn told the older woman. "Thank you for saying that. You've given me more to think about. Much more."

She had drifted away from him. Patrick felt it all that day. It wasn't just the issue of Marie, their small arguments. Bronwyn had refused to marry him, and it could only be because she didn't love him enough.

Later that morning, he and Louisa drove Wesley to school to see the presentation by the tarantula expert. In the classroom with Louisa, Patrick decided that looking at large hairy spiders was really stretching the limits of what was expected of a loving parent. His great-aunt had been far more interested in the spiders than he was.

Truthfully, it was hard to think about anything but Bronwyn, how much he loved her, the distance he felt between them. Night before last they'd made love, had lain blissfully in each other's arms in the rapt state of lovers who couldn't get enough of one another.

But she'd insisted upon sleeping alone the following night.

Patrick was glad that she'd been honest with him about her feelings. She hadn't just gone along with him, agreed to marry him because of Wesley. But it was too painful to remain at Fairchild Acres without the closeness he so wanted with her. If he left, he would miss her company. He would grieve the loss of her love. But he had told her his feelings, and she had answered with hers.

When she'd first come to Fairchild Acres, he'd wanted to somehow undo the past, to make Bronwyn admit that she'd made a mistake in choosing Ari Theodoros. Even more, he wanted to erase her rejection of him, to let it never have happened. He wanted to have always been her first choice.

And now— Well, she'd told him he would be her first choice now—after her desire to be alone, to retain her freedom.

The Bronwyn he loved now was a different woman from the Bronwyn of his university days. He loved her as the mother of their son, loved the way he saw her parent Wesley. He loved the vulnerability he saw in her now, something that had been kept more carefully under wraps when they were younger. He loved watching her find herself, express her nature through her work at the fitness center. She was coming into her own being, and perhaps he loved that most of all.

But what tension she must be under now. She'd taken no pleasure in rejecting him again. And he could sense the pressure she was under. She might feel that she should marry him, or at least remain his lover, if she wanted to stay at Fairchild Acres. And now this place was Wesley's home. Bronwyn wouldn't want to uproot her son, not now that he'd found a measure of security, now that he was surrounded by love in a wholesome environment.

She wouldn't want to take Wesley away from Louisa.

Patrick didn't want that, either. Fairchild Acres was Wesley's home. He was settled in school in the Hunter Valley.

For the rest of the day, as he handled both his own work, managing investments online, and the business related to Fairchild Acres, Patrick considered his situation with Bronwyn. The longer he thought about it, the clearer the answer became to him.

After all, he already had a place in Sydney.

He would come to Fairchild Acres frequently to visit, and Wesley—and Bronwyn, if she liked—could come to Sydney to see him.

It was the only right thing to do, because they couldn't both live here, together but separate. Well, he couldn't. He loved her, was in love with her. He would desire her, he would want her to love him, and she would feel that love as pressure.

No, there was only the one answer.

Strangely, it didn't make him miserable. It made him comfortable because he knew it was right.

Bronwyn must feel crowded by his love for her, by his yearning for a commitment from her.

He had to remove that stress from her.

Once he'd resolved that problem, he put in a call to Dylan to see if the detective could learn anything useful about Marie and Reynard, but he got the answering machine and decided not to leave a message.

Maybe he was wrong about Marie.

And what right had he to stir the pot when he would likely be returning to Sydney soon?

At midafternoon, he opened a beer and stepped out onto the porch, looking toward the road. Bronwyn. She was just heading toward the drive, starting her walk to the bus stop to meet Wesley, who had felt well enough to remain in school and asked to be allowed to ride the bus home with his friends. "Friends" had been the magic word for Patrick, and he'd relented and explained to Bronwyn when he and Louisa returned to Fairchild Acres.

Now, he left his beer bottle on the table close to where he'd been sitting and called her name.

She glanced up, and Patrick came down the steps and strode across the lawn to meet her.

I have to say it, he thought. Why not now?

"Mind if I join you?"

"No." But she smiled uncertainly, and doubts crashed through him.

Was that reserve he saw? Was it love? Or was it simply fear of the dilemma he represented for her?

"Bronwyn, I think I'm making things a bit difficult for you here."

"What?" She stopped walking and stared.

Well, she might look baffled, but Patrick had made his decision. The sense of its rightness remained with him.

"I think my being here is hemming you in. I'm in love with you, and I want to marry you, to be with you always. But you've given me a different answer, and I accept that. Wesley's settled here, you have a job and a home, and Louisa loves you both. I imagine you feel pressure to leave, or if not, to be my lover for all the wrong reasons."

She said nothing, only began walking again, her reaction veiled behind her eyes.

He wanted to know what she felt hearing his words. Yet he wasn't sure her feelings, whatever they were, had the power to alter his resolve. He had made a decision about what was best for all of them.

Bronwyn did not love him enough; it was that simple.

"So I've decided to go back to Sydney."

He didn't know what reaction he'd been hoping for. A gasp of astonishment? A show of tears? A cry of disappointment?

He received none of them.

She simply walked beside him and finally asked, "How will Louisa feel about that?"

"I think she'll see the necessity for the move."

Bronwyn had no doubt that he was right. If Louisa understood anything it was the need for decisions like this. She would be concerned about Wesley's welfare; Wesley was the one whom Louisa would want to remain at Fairchild Acres, no matter what, because she wouldn't want to see the boy uprooted.

Bronwyn looked up at Patrick. "I don't think Wesley will like it."

"He'll adjust," Patrick said equably.

"He'll go to visit you?" Bronwyn asked.

"With your permission. And I'll be back here frequently."

Bronwyn considered everything Patrick was saying. "You're doing this because…?"

"Bronwyn, you understand why."

She did. He was granting her freedom, letting her choose, and she was more grateful than she knew how to say.

"Patrick," she whispered.

"Yes?"

"Thank you."

Beside her, he swallowed. She felt it and saw it, and her own eyes stung.

The repeat rejection. The thing he hadn't wanted to experience again. She wanted to scream, *Patrick, I love you! Believe that I love you.* But it was not fair to say such things to him when she'd said she wouldn't marry him, when she wasn't sure of anything but the gratitude and love she felt for him and the choice he was making, a choice that allowed her to choose.

She said again, "Thank you." Then added, "And thank you for being Wesley's father."

Patrick blinked away any emotion. "I'll explain it to him," he said, "in a way he can understand."

Abruptly, Bronwyn made the decision to let him be the one to tell Wesley. "Thank you," she said again, wanting to take his hand.

Knowing that she should not.

Not now.

"I'll get you the computer so you can find the photographs you need online," Patrick told Wesley as the boy discussed his after-school plans, which included tarantula-related homework.

Bronwyn hugged Wesley and said, "And I have an appointment at the fitness center." With Crystal, for a one-on-one Pilates class.

She walked away after one smiling glance back at them.

Patrick watched her go. "Hey, buddy," he said to Wesley, who looked ready to go upstairs and change out of his school uniform. "I have some news for you."

Wesley looked up with an expression that reminded Patrick of Bronwyn. Patrick felt his heart breaking again.

He had gone from shock to anger to wanting vengeance when Bronwyn had chosen Ari over him. But the truth was that he'd been hurt. Under all the resentment, this pain had lurked. And now he was experiencing it once more.

Bronwyn did love him. He knew that. But she might not love him enough to want to be his wife.

"I'm moving back to Sydney, Wesley."

Wesley stared up at him with an expression of horror. "But you're my dad."

The words stabbed Patrick. "I am," he managed to say. "And I love you and your mother, but your mother needs a little space from me. It's not her decision," he said quickly. "It's mine. It's something I'm doing as a gift to her. By being good to your mother, I'm being good to you, too."

"I don't see that," Wesley said.

"I hope you come to understand it in time. You'll visit me in Sydney, and I'll see you here. Every weekend at the least," he said, knowing it to be a promise, a solemn vow to his son.

But tears had welled in Wesley's eyes.

"Oh, hell," said Patrick, and he embraced the child, who was suddenly sobbing. He longed to tell Wesley that this move was his last gambit, the only way he knew to win Bronwyn.

But telling Wesley that wouldn't be fair to Bronwyn, who, likely as not, would never choose to marry Patrick. He said, "Wesley, your mum and I love each other, and we're going to keep loving each other and being good friends." This, at least, should be possible, especially after they'd had a little space from each other, giving him time to recover.

If he ever did.

Who are you kidding, Patrick? What other woman have you ever loved as you love her?

He couldn't think about it, about the reality of leaving Bronwyn, the possibility of her falling in love with someone else, marrying someone else again. But he had to give her the room to choose.

Wesley's tears wet his shirt front, drenching the fabric.

"Sydney," Louisa said when Patrick had told her of his plans. "Away from Bronwyn and Wesley."

"To give Bronwyn space," he said. "I can't force her into marrying me by giving her no other choice. And in staying here, I feel as though that's what I'm doing, behaving indecently."

Louisa gave a sad smile. "I think you do understand her, Patrick. I hope you understand yourself, as well."

"What do you mean?" They sat in Louisa's parlor after Wesley and Bronwyn had both gone up to bed.

"I mean," Louisa said, "that I hope you will forgive Bronwyn if she lets you go."

"If she doesn't love me the same way that I love her," he replied, "that's nothing she can help, Louisa."

Louisa nodded. She walked toward Patrick, moving unevenly with her cane, and sat beside him on the Victorian love seat. "You are dear to me, Patrick Stafford. You are family, and Fairchild Acres is your home forever, as it is Megan's. The two of you mean more to me than I can say. I'm terribly glad that Wesley is here, but I will miss you."

"I'll be back frequently to visit." He tried to keep the catch out of his voice. But Louisa was elderly. She could be taken from him at any time.

That night as Louisa got ready for bed, she contemplated Patrick and Bronwyn. Patrick had changed. He no longer seemed the brash, arrogant man who had all but tried to force himself on Bronwyn when she'd first arrived.

Yet Bronwyn had rejected him once already. Though Louisa approved of Patrick's action in giving Bronwyn her space and independence, she feared for Bronwyn, feared for her choice of independence over love.

The terrible grief was with her. How could more

than sixty years have passed and yet she sometimes felt the loss as though it was yesterday?

The regret was something of which she never spoke.

And of course she never spoke of her child.

Ghastly. Ghastly to remember.

But her pain might be of value to someone else, to someone with a chance at love, a chance that had never truly been Louisa's.

Yes, she must speak of it.

The next morning, after Wesley left for school, Patrick began packing his car. He wouldn't leave while Wesley was at school, knowing Wesley would want a hug goodbye. He'd already promised to see his son the following weekend, back at Fairchild Acres.

As he was carrying a box full of work files out of the house, Bronwyn came upstairs, having just finished teaching her morning yoga class. Louisa emerged from her office, threw an unreadable look at Patrick, and said, "Bronwyn, could you please come here and help me with something?"

Here was the parlor. Patrick wondered why Louisa looked so grave. He said, "Do you need me?"

"Bronwyn," she repeated, but Bronwyn was already hurrying toward Louisa.

Bronwyn followed Louisa into her parlor, and Louisa shut the door behind her and made her way to the love seat, where she carefully sat. She nodded at the space beside her, inviting Bronwyn to sit there, which Bronwyn did.

This is about Patrick, she thought. She doesn't want Patrick to go.

And he was going because of Bronwyn.

Everything roiled inside her, turning her decisions on their heads. Patrick's determination to leave, to let her be, had changed something in her heart, deepened her love for him, made it more clear to her.

"I am going to tell you something in confidence," Louisa said. "I've never spoken of this to a soul."

Bronwyn blinked.

"Many people wonder why I banished my own sister from Fairchild Acres."

Bronwyn's heart seemed to still. Everything within her was poised for Louisa's next words. Why is she telling me?

But Bronwyn did know why. In some way, she reminded Louisa of herself. Louisa had said as much. That fact touched and flattered Bronwyn. She was glad to be like Louisa, wanted to be like her.

"When I was a teenager," Louisa said, "I became pregnant."

Bronwyn's breath did not change. She remained motionless.

"I went away. That's what we did in those days." A pause. "There is no need to go into details. My baby died in childbirth."

Bronwyn let out a small cry, unable to help herself. As she imagined Louisa's pain, her own eyes filled with tears, and she was shocked to see a sheen in Louisa's eyes. It was no surprise that after decades the memory of a child's death could still make a mother cry. But Louisa? She was so strong, believed by so many to be indomitable.

"Then I learned that my sister was involved with the man I loved, the father of my baby. I could not bear to have them at Fairchild Acres, and when the estate came under my control I asked her to leave. With the man I loved.

"And this is the thing, Bronwyn," she rushed on. "I did not fight for my love. I did not make my love known. I let it go. And that choice has changed my entire life, changed me, and not for the better." She withdrew a lace-edged handkerchief from one of her trouser pockets and methodically dried her eyes. "Anyhow, that's it. Don't make my mistakes, Bronwyn."

Bronwyn felt a chill within her. Patrick was packing.

Patrick had forgiven her for choosing someone else over him once.

And for refusing him a second time.

Now he was granting her freedom, freedom to let him go.

I can't let him go.

She knew it, knew it with certainty.

There had never been a man for her like Patrick, never would be.

She whispered, "Thank you, Louisa." Half blind,

half mad, she rose from the love seat and rushed to the door, throwing it open.

Where was he? He wouldn't leave without saying goodbye to Wesley. He couldn't be gone already.

She searched the bottom story, then rushed up the stairs to find him in his office, selecting books to put in a box.

How am I going to tell him? she thought. How can I tell him when he is doing all this for me?

"Patrick," she said, grasping the doorjambs, holding on tight. "Patrick."

He straightened up, came toward her.

She looked up into his eyes and made the words come out, the words that stole her freedom and gave her a new freedom, words that would bring her a new life. "Patrick, I love you. Please don't go. Unless you're the one with doubts. I have none. None at all."

His eyes reminded her of Louisa's as he wrapped his arms around her, pulled her against him, whispered into her hair, "Are you sure, Bronwyn? That you want to marry me, live with me, be my love and my wife till death takes one of us?"

She clasped him tightly. "I'm sure." And she added softly, "Now that's what I call a decent proposal."

He laughed, and she looked up to see the laughter in his eyes and met his mouth with hers.

"Shall we tell Louisa the good news?" he asked.

"I think she deserves to know first thing," Bronwyn

told him. "And then there's someone else who's going to be ecstatic."

"There certainly is," Patrick said, holding her close, as though he would never let her go. "We'll take him out for a ride after school, maybe take a picnic and celebrate."

Yes, there were so many people to tell, Bronwyn reflected. Marie and Helena. Megan and Dylan. And most of all, most of all Wesley. They were all her family. Because for the first time in her life, Bronwyn was truly home.

Silhouette Desire kicks off 2009 with
MAN OF THE MONTH,
*a yearlong program featuring incredible heroes
by stellar authors.*

When navy SEAL Hunter Cabot returns home for
some much-needed R & R, he discovers he's a
married man. There's just one problem: he's never
met his "bride."

*Enjoy this sneak peek at Maureen Child's
AN OFFICER AND A MILLIONAIRE.
Available January 2009 from Silhouette Desire.*

One

Hunter Cabot, Navy SEAL, had a healing bullet wound in his side, thirty days' leave and, apparently, a wife he'd never met.

On the drive into his hometown of Springville, California, he stopped for gas at Charlie Evans's service station. That's where the trouble started.

"Hunter! Man, it's good to see you! Margie didn't tell us you were coming home."

"Margie?" Hunter leaned back against the front fender of his black pickup truck and winced as his side gave a small twinge of pain. Silently then, he watched as the man he'd known since high school filled his tank.

Charlie grinned, shook his head and pumped gas. "Guess your wife was lookin' for a little 'alone' time with you, huh?"

"My—" Hunter couldn't even say the word. *Wife?* He didn't have a wife. "Look, Charlie..."

"Don't blame her, of course," his friend said with a wink as he finished up and put the gas cap back on. "You being gone all the time with the SEALs must be hard on the ol' love life."

He'd never had any complaints, Hunter thought, frowning at the man still talking a mile a minute. "What're you—"

"Bet Margie's anxious to see you. She told us all about that R & R trip you two took to Bali." Charlie's dark brown eyebrows lifted and wiggled.

"Charlie..."

"Hey, it's okay, you don't have to say a thing, man."

What the hell could he say? Hunter shook his head, paid for his gas and as he left, told himself Charlie was just losing it. Maybe the guy had been smelling gas fumes too long.

But as it turned out, it wasn't just Charlie. Stopped at a red light on Main Street, Hunter glanced out his window to smile at Mrs. Harker, his second-grade teacher who was now at least a hundred years old. In the middle of the crosswalk, the old lady stopped and shouted, "Hunter Cabot, you've got yourself a wonderful wife. I hope you appreciate her."

Scowling now, he only nodded at the old woman—the only teacher who'd ever scared the crap out of him. What the hell was going on here? Was everyone but him nuts?

His temper beginning to boil, he put up with a few more comments about his "wife" on the drive through town before finally pulling into the wide, circular drive leading to the Cabot mansion. Hunter didn't have a clue what was going on, but he planned to get to the bottom of it. Fast.

He grabbed his duffel bag, stalked into the house and paid no attention to the housekeeper, who ran at him, fluttering both hands. "Mr. Hunter!"

"Sorry, Sophie," he called out over his shoulder as he took the stairs two at a time. "Need a shower, then we'll talk."

He marched down the long, carpeted hallway to the rooms that were always kept ready for him. In his suite, Hunter tossed the duffel down and stopped dead. The shower in his bathroom was running. His *wife?*

Anger and curiosity boiled in his gut, creating a churning mass that had him moving forward without even thinking about it. He opened the bathroom door to a wall of steam and the sound of a woman singing—off-key. Margie, no doubt.

Well, if she was his wife… Hunter walked across the room, yanked the shower door open and stared in at a curvy, naked, temptingly wet woman.

She whirled to face him, slapping her arms across her naked body while she gave a short, terrified scream.

Hunter smiled. "Hi, honey. I'm home."

* * * * *

Be sure to look for
AN OFFICER AND A MILLIONAIRE
by USA TODAY *bestselling author Maureen Child.*
Available January 2009 from Silhouette Desire.

CELEBRATE
60 YEARS
OF PURE READING PLEASURE
WITH **HARLEQUIN®**!

We'll be spotlighting a different series
every month throughout 2009
to celebrate our 60th anniversary.
Look for Silhouette Desire® in January!

MAN of the
MONTH

Collect all 12 books in the Silhouette Desire®
Man of the Month continuity, starting in
January 2009 with *An Officer and a Millionaire*
by *USA TODAY* bestselling author
Maureen Child.

*Look for one new Man of the Month title
every month in 2009!*

Thoroughbred Legacy

The purse is set and the stakes are high...
Romance, scandal and glamour set in the
exhilarating world of horse-racing!

The Legacy continues with book #9

DARCI'S PRIDE
by Jenna Mills

Six years ago, Tyler Preston was on top of the equestrian world...
until one disastrous night nearly ruined him. Now, after years
of hard work, his beloved Lochlain Racing has reemerged. Then
Darci Parnell—the woman who'd cost Tyler everything—walks
into his office and changes his life forever.

**Look for DARCI'S PRIDE
in December 2008 wherever books are sold.**

Thoroughbred Legacy

The purse is set and the stakes are high…
Romance, scandal and glamour in the
exhilarating world of horse racing!

The Legacy continues with book #10

BREAKING FREE

by Loreth Anne White

Aussie cop Dylan Hastings believes in things that are *real*.
Family. Integrity. Justice. And he knows from bitter experience
that the wrong woman can destroy it all. So when art dealer
Megan Stafford walks into his life, he knows trouble's not far
behind.

***Look for BREAKING FREE
in December 2008 wherever books are sold.***

Home to Texas and straight to the altar!

Luke: The Cowboy Heir
by
PATRICIA THAYER

Luke never saw himself returning to
Mustang Valley. But as a Randell the land
is in his blood and is calling him back…
And blond beauty Tess Meyers is waiting
for Luke Randell's return….

Available January 2009
wherever you buy books.

REQUEST YOUR FREE BOOKS!

2 FREE NOVELS PLUS 2 FREE GIFTS!

SPECIAL EDITION®

Life, Love and Family!

YES! Please send me 2 FREE Silhouette Special Edition® novels and my 2 FREE gifts (gifts are worth about $10). After receiving them, if I don't wish to receive any more books, I can return the shipping statement marked "cancel." If I don't cancel, I will receive 6 brand-new novels every month and be billed just $4.24 per book in the U.S. or $4.99 per book in Canada, plus 25¢ shipping and handling per book and applicable taxes, if any*. That's a savings of at least 15% off the cover price! I understand that accepting the 2 free books and gifts places me under no obligation to buy anything. I can always return a shipment and cancel at any time. Even if I never buy another book from Silhouette, the two free books and gifts are mine to keep forever.

235 SDN EEYU   335 SDN EEY6

Name	(PLEASE PRINT)

Address	Apt. #

City	State/Prov.	Zip/Postal Code

Signature (if under 18, a parent or guardian must sign)

Mail to the **Silhouette Reader Service:**
IN U.S.A.: P.O. Box 1867, Buffalo, NY 14240-1867
IN CANADA: P.O. Box 609, Fort Erie, Ontario L2A 5X3

Not valid to current subscribers of Silhouette Special Edition books.

Want to try two free books from another line?
Call 1-800-873-8635 or visit www.morefreebooks.com.

* Terms and prices subject to change without notice. N.Y. residents add applicable sales tax. Canadian residents will be charged applicable provincial taxes and GST. Offer not valid in Quebec. This offer is limited to one order per household. All orders subject to approval. Credit or debit balances in a customer's account(s) may be offset by any other outstanding balance owed by or to the customer. Please allow 4 to 6 weeks for delivery. Offer available while quantities last.

Your Privacy: Silhouette is committed to protecting your privacy. Our Privacy Policy is available online at www.eHarlequin.com or upon request from the Reader Service. From time to time we make our lists of customers available to reputable third parties who may have a product or service of interest to you. If you would prefer we not share your name and address, please check here. ☐

SSE08R

You're invited to join our Tell Harlequin Reader Panel!

By joining our new reader panel you will:

- Receive Harlequin® books—they are FREE and yours to keep with no obligation to purchase anything!
- Participate in fun online surveys
- Exchange opinions and ideas with women just like you
- Have a say in our new book ideas and help us publish the best in women's fiction

In addition, you will have a chance to win great prizes and receive special gifts!
See Web site for details. Some conditions apply.
Space is limited.

To join, visit us at
www.TellHarlequin.com.